BLIZZARD WARNING

The Damaged Climate Series Book 3

J.R. TATE

Rusty Bucket Publishing

Cover art by J.R. Tate

Created with Vellum

ALSO BY J.R. TATE

Respect the Wind Series

Fury - Book One

Rage - Book 2

The Defiants Series

Inception - Book One

Captive - Book Two

Desist - Book Three

The Firefighter Heroes Series

Through Smoke - Book One

Backfire - Book Two

Fire Escape - Book Three

The Gifted Curse Series

Beckoning Souls - Book One

Wayward Souls - Book Two

ALSO BY J.R. TATE (CONTINUED)

Stand-Alone Novels

Fade to Gray

Reformed

Keep the Wolves Away

Dangerous Betrayal

Murphy's War

CHAPTER ONE

"Does it look like rain?"

Ryan glanced to his right, shaking his head toward Steve. "No. Just Virga showers again. Nature's slap in the face." He stood on the shovel, forcing it into the parched ground, putting as much weight on the metal as he could. It only sunk in a few inches before he hit the hard dirt just beneath the topsoil.

"Virga showers," Steve repeated, clicking his tongue. "If only we could figure out a way to get something up that high to pull that moisture down."

"It's next to impossible but sure would be helpful," Ryan replied. "How's the corn look? We need to make a run down to the river to get some water?"

"It couldn't hurt to do a little. It's growing tall considering that it's not getting as much water as it normally requires."

Ryan grabbed the wheelbarrow and pushed it through the rows of vegetation that were faring a tad better than he had anticipated. The cotton, though a very small crop, was popping out of the ground nicely, and the tomatoes, corn, and other vegetables were proving strong during the high temperatures, windburn, and dust storms that had continued to plague the area. None of the plants had produced blossoms yet, and with temperatures not getting below the nineties at night, it might be too hot for them to mature enough to make any blossoms.

Striding down the hill, Ryan stopped at the bank of the river and cringed at the sight in front of him. With days without precipitation reaching a record, the water supply was feeling the strain. He noticed a line where the water once was, the land above it yellow and brown from drought, below green from recent moisture. Soon it would transition to the ugly desert colors. The water still flowed and was deep, though not near as plentiful as it usually was this time of year. The lake it flowed into was in decent shape but in some areas stagnant, which meant a greater chance of catching something that contaminated their water supply.

They filled the two wheelbarrows with water. Getting them back up to the pasture was challenging and Ryan tried hard not to slosh any off the side. When they got to the top of the hill, both he and Steve took cups and poured them down the rows of corn – the ground sucked up the water like a sponge that had been sitting under a sink for years.

"Are you still working on an irrigation system?" Steve asked as he patted some water on his neck.

Ryan had a good plan for a drip irrigation system powered by gravity. The hard part was gathering the materials to get it finished. He needed old piping, which he could find in wreckage around houses and near the fire station. He also needed something strong enough to make holes in the thick metal. If he could come across some PVC pipe that hadn't been destroyed, it'd be perfect.

"I've got it going but I need some pipe. I'm going to put holes in the sides and flow the water through, running it downhill. It won't evaporate as fast as pouring it directly on the ground and plants. I'm almost done. Just delayed due to the lack of supplies. Chief Rayburn said he might have some stuff that was salvaged from the firehouse but there's no rushing that man. There's no sense of urgency with him lately."

Steve didn't reply and Ryan followed his gaze toward the mountains, his stomach sinking at the sight in the distance. It had been several weeks since they had been bothered by the group of looters and though Ryan knew they weren't finished, he hoped he was wrong, and they would be gone for good.

"This can't be happening," Steve whispered.

"They're not going to let it go. They want revenge for killing one of their men." Ryan dumped the rest of the water down the rows of plants. If they left it sitting, it'd evaporate and be a waste. "Let's get back to the shelter. Maybe if they don't see us, they won't come. They might have something else on their mind." It was wishful thinking but the only thinking Ryan would allow.

Running back to the cellar, Ryan motioned for everyone to gather. He noticed Ty and Cecilia playing on some old fire equipment that a few of the guys had made into a playground. Cecilia's eyebrow arched and her shoulders slumped – she knew exactly what was happening. Picking up Ty, she joined the small group that had formed at the cellar door. There weren't many survivors left but the people there were priceless. Ryan made note that Chief Rayburn wasn't there, nor were a few of the other firefighters.

They had cut down on the rescue teams going out to find people – it had been months since the initial tornadoes had come through. Anyone missing was now deemed a casualty and they could no longer exhaust resources on trying to find them. Now they turned their focus to salvage missions in hopes to bring back beneficial supplies to help Harper Springs. Hopefully, they would all make it back before the looters cornered them, wherever the men might be.

"What is it, Ryan?" Cecilia scooted close to him. "I know that look. You're worried about something."

"We saw them. The looters. They're back in the area." Ryan took a deep breath to try and gain composure. The short jog from the pasture felt like he ran a marathon, the heat heavy on his shoulders as if he were carrying another person.

"Are they coming this way?" Mindy chimed in, her small frame almost covered by people standing in front of her.

"It's hard to say. They were near the mountain range in the west. We didn't give them a chance to spot us before we came back here."

"The fact that they have taken this long to come back and attack is a mystery," someone yelled and Ryan agreed.

"How are we on ammunition?" Ryan asked Steve.

"With the lack of gunpowder, we are unable to recycle a lot of the shell casings, but we do still have them gathered up."

"If we're running low, the looters are bound to be running low too. Where would we be able to find gunpowder?" Ryan thought for a second, glancing out at the group of people who were waiting for a plan that Ryan didn't have. "Didn't Farmer Johnson keep his gun-making stuff in his cellar?" He turned to his father, hoping he'd know.

Darryl didn't answer and Mindy interrupted. "We don't have time for that, Ryan. If they're on their way, they'll be here within the hour. What are we gonna do?"

"Everyone get down in the cellar. Gather up all the guns and weapons you have. Even if it's not a weapon but can be used as one, get it. Don't come up to ground level unless we say. They know this is where we are living but if enough of us meet them with gunfire, they might think twice." He opened the door, and everyone went down inside. When had he become the leader? Chief Rayburn had seemed to step into that void, but he was missing in action.

Cecilia stopped at the edge of the stairs, clutching Ty close to her chest. "Where are you going? You're not coming down there with us?"

"No. I need to go scout. I need to make sure they're coming this way before we completely panic."

"Didn't we agree that we aren't going to split up anymore?"

She didn't even attempt to prevent Ty from hearing. The child's expression was blank – he was becoming numb to their new way of life. That was both good and bad.

"We did but there's no one else around to do this." Ryan didn't have time to argue. It was apparent by her creased brow and hard glare that her patience was gone. He couldn't fault her for that. This was no way to live.

"Just make sure that while you're off playing hero for everyone you don't forget that you have a son who needs his father. I'm not sure what you're trying to prove but your luck will eventually run out, Ryan." She took her mom's arm and guided her down the stairs.

Her words stung and Ryan ducked his head. She didn't mean it. Emotions were running high, and he couldn't take it to heart. He watched her go down the stairs until he couldn't see her anymore. Darryl was next to go in and he clapped his hand on Ryan's shoulder, shaking his head. He didn't have to say anything – he spoke so much with just his body language. Everyone was tired, hungry, and ready for this to be over.

"I won't be gone long, Dad," Ryan said. "I hope she doesn't stay mad at me for this."

"She won't. Get going. I'll make sure she understands."

Ryan hugged him and jogged to where they were keeping the horses. They had made corrals out of rope to keep the animals from running off. With the shifts in weather, it was nothing short of a miracle that the horses hadn't been lost in the middle of it all.

Steve was behind him, and they rode north. There was an open valley where they could hide low to watch and hopefully not be spotted. The sweat fell down Ryan's face, stinging his eyes. When he licked his lips, he could taste the salt on his skin. The sun beat down on them, baking them as they rode across the thirsty land.

Ryan's mind raced with everything – Cecilia was frustrated. He tried to have empathy for her. How would he feel if it was her going off in every direction with no way of checking in on her safety? He would be less than amused at it so he couldn't fault her for acting the way she was. But he also couldn't just sit around when there was imminent danger all around them. He had to protect his family and the rest of the survivors left in Harper Springs.

Steve waved toward him, pointing to the area where they planned to hide to spy on the group of misfits. There was an uprooted tree that was still big enough to tie the horses to. Crouching, Ryan squinted as he watched the group of looters on the horizon. It was the perfect location to spy but he still feared they could see them. With so many trees ripped up or dying from the drought, the view wasn't hindered by them, making the visibility miles ahead.

"Well, they're not moving anymore. Which doesn't mean anything." Ryan observed, lying flat on his stomach, shielding his eyes. "They could just be resting their horses or setting up camp for the night. Or they could be playing mind games with us. They're not stupid. They know we're watching."

"Do you want to stay here all night to watch?"

"I can't do that. Cecilia would send out a search party and kill me herself if I did."

"Yeah, Mindy would probably do the same thing to me," Steve replied, sipping from a canteen that he offered to Ryan.

Taking it, he gulped it, the cool water refreshing. "That's getting serious, huh?" Ryan wiped his mouth with the back of his hand and gave the canteen back to Steve.

"As serious as it could be considering the pile of shit we're in right now. Not exactly under conditions where I can romanticize with a lady."

Ryan kept his eyes on the looters, but the small talk was refreshing, like they weren't scouting out a possible threat to their lives. Like he and Steve were just out on a camping trip for the weekend.

"Well, we do need to replenish the population." Ryan winked

and arched his eyebrow, laughing. It felt good. It was an emotion he hadn't experienced in a long time.

"I should kick your ass for that, Ryan."

Steve's cheeks reddened and Ryan left it alone after that. He didn't want to let his guard down and he had done his job of embarrassing the man. His mind quickly switched back to the current situation – two men in the group were on horses, both angled down the hill. Ryan was having a hard time seeing everything, but they were riding away, a cloud of dust billowing up behind the horses, which meant they were traveling fast.

Propping himself up on his elbows, Ryan sat up and checked the revolver in his pocket. It was just a six-shooter. Along with the large Bowie knife he was carrying, those were the only two decent weapons he had on him.

"Steve, you happen to grab anything that might help us back at base camp?"

He slid a nine-millimeter handgun from the homemade holster on his hip. "Magazine is full – sixteen shots ready to go."

"Good. We're gonna need them. Two men are on the move, and I want to follow them, see where they're going."

Saddling up, they made a wide circle around the valley. They had to take the long way to avoid being spotted by the rest of the looters. It was tricky, keeping the two riders in their sights and steering clear of the large group. It would be convenient to have eyes on the backs of their heads. As conspicuous as Ryan felt they were being, it was probably not as incognito as he was hoping it'd be. He had to think about the chance that they would trap them. After all, he was involved in killing one of their leaders.

Ryan slowed his horse when he realized they had turned south. Harper Springs was east of their location. Holding his hand up, he halted Steve's horse and the dust around them settled.

"Something tells me we shouldn't follow them just yet. They're going away from town. The main band of them are staying west up near the mountains. And it's getting dark. I don't want to get cornered and I sure as hell don't want to stay out here after the sun goes down. We didn't bring any lanterns or flashlights. We could stumble right up on them and then what?"

"I agree."

"We'll just have to set up watch like we've been doing. Everyone should be back for the evening, and we can all run short shifts so we can get some rest."

Ryan checked all four directions one last time to make sure. Everything was quiet – almost too quiet, and the hair on the back of his neck stood up. They were vulnerable and unprepared. Directing the horse east, they trotted back to town. There was no doubt in his mind that they had been spotted, which might not be such a bad thing. He wanted them to know he was watching - they wouldn't catch them off guard, and that they were preparing for whatever might come. He could at least fake it, even if they were in no way ready for a battle.

Cecilia met him at the top of the stairs, her eyes red and swollen. If she attempted to hide the fact that she had been crying, she wasn't doing a good job. Reaching out, Ryan caressed her hand, and to his surprise, she allowed it.

"I figured I was the last person you'd want to talk to right now," Ryan said, following her down the stairs to their far corner in the back of the cellar. Lanterns lit up the darkness and even their surplus of propane and lamp oil were running low. Soon, if they were down in the shelter, it'd be complete darkness, used only to sleep in. They'd have to find other ways above ground to shower and cook, and an area for medical to be able to perform surgeries and well-checks.

Cecilia sat on the edge of her cot, the springs squeaking from her weight. Glancing over at Ty, she pulled up the blanket around him and heaved a deep sigh.

"Ryan, I'm sorry I blew up earlier. You didn't deserve that."

"I kinda did, Cecilia."

"No, you're doing what you need to do. I trust you. I lost my father. I don't want to lose you too."

Sitting beside her on the cot, Ryan pulled her in for a side hug, resting his chin on the top of her head. By the way her body quivered, he could tell she was crying, and when she buried her face in his chest, he felt the warmth of her tears soak through the thin fabric of his t-shirt. How could this be their reality now? It was the twenty-first century, and they were having to live like cavemen.

"I'm sorry if I keep making you worry. I just... I can't sit around and wait for them to attack. I have to make sure we're protected."

She looked up and wiped the tears from her cheeks. "I know. Which is why I'm apologizing. It's who you are and it's why I love you. You've always taken care of us. I can't expect you to not do it now." Adjusting her weight, she turned to face him, intertwining her fingers in his. "What did y'all see? Are they coming?"

"I don't know," Ryan replied. On the cot beside Ty, Cecilia's mother was sound asleep. It was good to see her getting rest. For the first few nights back in Harper Springs, she cried all the time and hardly said anything.

"You don't know?" Cecilia cocked her head to the side.

"A couple of guys split off from the group. Went south. It could be a diversion. They could be scoping out another place to loot. Hell, I don't know. But we have to keep a watch on them. They know what we have. They know what they can steal from us." He rubbed his eyes and they burned under his lids. What he'd give for a hot shower, a cold beer, and a complete night's rest. Those things would probably never happen again.

"Do they outnumber us?"

"Hard to say. I think we have more if you include the women and children. We just have to stay together."

"What's the plan right now?"

Ryan leaned back against the dirt wall, his body sinking into it. If he could get his mind to shut down for two seconds, he'd be asleep as soon as he closed his eyes.

"Steve is taking first watch. We'll just have someone up there keeping an eye on things. Not sure how beneficial it'll be, considering they can attack from any direction they want. It's about the only thing we can do right now. I guess it's for peace of mind. We need to stay alert just in case."

"Right. It's basically out of your hands, so how about you lay back and get some sleep? I'm sure if something goes down, you won't sleep through it anyway."

Ryan didn't refute her idea and slid in behind her, wrapping his arms around her waist. It was the only time they got to be alone, and he nuzzled her neck, kissing a trail up to her hair. As predicted, his physical exhaustion trumped his mental worry, and he dozed off into a deep sleep.

CHAPTER TWO

Ryan felt comfortable. He could hear voices chatting around him, but it was as if they were in a tunnel. He forced his eyes open and everything around him was blurry. Blinking to clear his vision, Ryan sat up. Others around him were awake and moving around, and the strong scent of coffee wafted toward him. Ty was at the table where the finger foods were, skimming over his minimal choices. Cecilia handed him a foil package and he skipped off to a group where some other kids were.

He didn't know what time it was, but from the fresh scent of coffee and how many people were awake, it was morning. Steve was chatting with Mindy and Chief Rayburn was acting like a politician, speaking to two other guys near the stairs.

"Sleeping Beauty awakens." Cecilia handed him a cup of instant coffee, the steam swirling upward.

"What time is it?" His voice sounded rough, and his throat felt sore.

"Around seven AM. You hungry?"

"Did they come to get me last night to..."

"No. You didn't move. As soon as you fell asleep, you were out." Cecilia smiled.

"I was supposed to take watch after Steve. Why didn't they come get me?"

Just as Cecilia was about to respond, Steve walked by and Ryan grabbed his arm, stopping him. "Why didn't you wake me up last night? I was supposed to help."

"You looked way too comfortable. And besides, I tried. If it wasn't for the fact that you were breathing, we could've chalked you up as a casualty. Nothing was getting you out of that bed last night. And don't worry – it's under control. They're still in the same spot in the foothills of the mountains. They haven't moved."

"Yet," Ryan replied, finishing his coffee. He put the cup on a nearby table to use for later. "You do a walk-through? How's the pasture look?"

"I was just about do that. Run a comb through that mop of yours and we'll head that way."

They took the horses just in case they would need to trail somebody or run. With too many possibilities lurking, Ryan didn't want to take any chances and be left vulnerable away from the shelter. Keeping a gun on him was a common practice now but with ammunition running low, they'd have to be conservative on how or what they shot at. Hunting was important as well, and they'd eventually have to figure out how to start making their own bullets. He used to do it but without supplies, it'd be an added challenge.

When they got to the pasture, Ryan didn't see the group of looters on the foothill. Looking in every direction, his heart skipped a beat when he didn't spot them anywhere.

"Hey, Steve, do you see them?"

Steve shielded his eyes against the morning sun, looking directly at where they had camped the night before. "Nope."

"Shit. That could be good or bad."

"Where could they be?"

"I don't know. They're playing mind games with us. We could do one of two things, but neither is very appealing." Ryan lifted his baseball cap and swiped the sweat on his brow. His hair was plastered to his forehead, and he longed for cooler weather. Once a person who hated winter, he wouldn't mind a gentle snowfall coming through. It would be like heaven.

"What two choices do we have?" Steve asked, keeping his eyes on the foothills.

"We could go back to the shelter and just hope they're not planning something." He paused and took a sip of water, letting option one sink in, and then continued. "Or we could ride up to where they had camp and see if they left anything behind. Could be a trap. Could be nothing at all. We could be over-estimating the intelligence of them, but they've got revenge on their mind. A man is dangerous when he's looking for vengeance."

"You're right. Neither of those is very appealing," Steve acknowledged. "I saw we go scope it out. There aren't many places to hide with all the trees torn up. It doesn't appear that they are within a few miles. In and out. Make it quick."

Ryan surveyed their surroundings. It was like the looters had vanished into thin air. He hesitated – a part of him said no, don't go. It was a trap. They were going to get them right where they wanted them and then they'd be screwed. But he also couldn't just sit around and hope that they weren't closing in on the entire town for a surprise attack. He couldn't mull it over too long. Being apprehensive was making him look weak, and though Steve knew him, it was casting an ill light on him.

"Let's do it. But we need to let someone know back at the shelter. We need them to come look for us if we're not back by a certain time."

"Cecilia ain't gonna like this," Steve stated, arching his eyebrow.

"We won't tell her, Steve. Haven't you ever heard that it's easier to ask for forgiveness than permission? I live by that."

Steve laughed and dug the heel of his boot into the side of the horse. "I did, which is why I'm a divorced man now."

They made a quick trip to town and luck was on their side –

Darryl was at ground level, and he was alone. Ryan steadied the horse and told him their plan. It was no mystery that his father would immediately go tell Cecilia, but they'd be halfway to the foothills before she could even do anything about it.

"You sure this is a smart idea?" Darryl looked up at them, squinting. "Don't let Doug's ignorance cloud your judgment. The rest of those men probably have some common sense."

"We'll be quick."

"When should I send a search party out for you?"

Ryan looked up at the sun. By its position, it was almost eight AM, give or take a few minutes. "Give us an hour for safe measure. The hills aren't far, but I don't want you to freak out too soon and come guns blazing."

"Speaking of guns, are you well armed for this?"

"Sixteen shots in the nine-millimeter, I've got my six-shooter, my knife..."

"Take this." Darryl held up the old deer rifle he had used for as long as Ryan could remember. "It's easy to load, shoots straight, and is smooth." He tossed Ryan his ammunition belt. "I hope you don't have to use any of it."

"Me too. It'll be fine. We'll be right back."

Before Ryan could talk himself out of it, he and Steve ran the horses west. He felt guilty for not telling Cecilia. She had worried enough. She'd completely lose it if he made it a point to tell her and she was already angry with him.

On horseback, the travel time to the mountains would be just under ten to fifteen minutes. Ryan had to get into the habit of not running the animals at full speed – human beings weren't the only ones suffering from the erratic weather changes. And the horses had been going non-stop since everything had panned out, serving on rescues, and helping with the planting. He also had to make sure they'd have enough stamina to run in case they got put into a dangerous situation once they reached their destination.

Ryan made sure to keep checking behind them. Despite the

torn-up trees, there was still enough shrubbery for someone to hide in and jump out at them. It was playing out like an old west movie, and they were having to make sure there weren't renegade Indians waiting to attack and claim their scalps. The looters could have people anywhere, watching their every move. Complacency would get them killed. He gripped the reins tightly, the sweat on his palms dripping against the leather. A combination of heat and fear contributed to the moisture on his skin. There was no hiding it – this might not have been the best decision he had ever made.

They were close so they slowed their horses and Ryan continued to check their surroundings for scouts. If they got trapped, it'd be from the least obvious setup. Each crack of dry grass under the horse's hooves made him jump. The bastards were bold enough to hide in plain sight, and Ryan hoped he wasn't overlooking the obvious.

Sliding off the side of his horse, he kept it close just in case he had to get back on quickly. Steve did the same. There wasn't much to explore – a fire pit made of rocks, some soot, and burned wood from a campfire. That was the only evidence left behind by the group. With a survival mentality, everyone was in the mindset not to leave anything behind.

At first, he thought it was his imagination but when he heard the patter of footsteps and the crunch of the grass, Ryan knew someone had been close by but where did they go? His instincts were screaming at him to make a beeline back to town, but curiosity plagued him – he wanted to know what the looter's plans were. Their former campsite lent no clues to help.

"Looks like this is a bust," Ryan replied. "They've moved on and I wish to hell I knew where they were going."

"Did you hear that?" Steve stopped in his tracks, holding his hand up to stop them.

"No, what?"

"Shh!"

Ryan followed Steve's gaze. He was looking in the direction

where he heard the footsteps. A gust of wind howled past, kicking up some dust around them. And then he heard it – more footsteps, grass crunching, and twigs breaking. It was getting closer, and Ryan instinctively put his hand on the butt of his handgun. Ready to draw, he patiently waited for the person to reveal who they were. But no one came out. It fell silent. Someone was watching them. They weren't alone.

"We need to get the hell outta here," Ryan whispered, his heart beating so hard that he could almost see it through his shirt. He had already killed two men. He didn't want to have to kill another.

"What if it's someone who needs our help?"

"What if it's someone who wants to blow us away?" Ryan kept his palm on the gun, his fingers wrapping around the handle and releasing several times, a nervous tick he noticed he had developed through all of it. "Who's there?" He tried to hide the shaking in his voice but was unsuccessful. Probably not the smartest question to ask, either.

No response. No movement. Now Steve had Ryan second-guessing himself. What if it was a child? Or someone like Mindy? Handing the reins to Steve, he took a few steps forward, peering around a crevice in the side of the hill. On the other side, he saw two wild hogs. Neither had spotted him. If they had, they would either be attacking him or they'd run, but Ryan had them cornered. They were backed against the hill and the only way out was to run past him.

"Those things are dangerous," Steve muttered, edging in close to Ryan.

"Those things are going to be our dinner tonight." Ryan's mouth watered at the thought of roasted pork. The fact that the hogs weren't coming after them was enough evidence for Ryan to conclude that they weren't rabid. The rifle would prove to be the better weapon – his father had killed many deer with it.

Sliding it from the saddlebag, Ryan aimed. He'd have to shoot fast to get them both. As soon as the gunfire would ring out, they'd run. Resting his index finger on the trigger, he closed one eye, putting the cross hairs right on the closest boar to them. If he waited any longer, they'd spot him and be a harder target to hit.

Squeezing the trigger, the shot rang out, echoing against the mountains. As predicted, the other hog ran, and Ryan focused on it. Wasting no time, he pulled the trigger again. The animal fell to the ground with a hard thud, kicking up dust from the weight of his body. The first boar was lying on its side, the direct hit fatal. The second one was flopping around, squealing as it fought the pain searing through its body. Ryan trotted to it, shooting it in the head. It was best to put the animal out of its misery and within a split second, it fell motionless, their glossy eyes staring up at Ryan.

"The trip up here wasn't wasted, after all," Steve said as both men stood over Ryan's kill.

"No. We'll be eating well tonight," Ryan replied. "This will be enough to feed all of us." It'd be a nice change from the canned meat and fish they'd been living on.

"The tone of your voice says otherwise," Steve responded, patting him on the shoulder. "What gives?"

Ryan looked in every direction, but the view was stilted by the hills. "We still have those damn looters to think about. Poof, they're gone. And they'll be back."

"And we'll be ready." Steve knelt beside the boar. "Let's get these loaded up. We're looking at a little over two-hundred pounds of meat here. It'll be enough for a few meals."

Ryan helped Steve lift the first hog and draped it over the back of the horse. They'd have to ride slow with the added weight. The second hog wasn't quite as big but still a plentiful hunt that everyone back in Harper Springs would welcome with open arms.

Despite their good fortune, Ryan still couldn't shake the worry. They needed to find a way to protect the town. They could gather lumber from trees to build walls around the perimeter of the pasture and their shelter. Right now, Harper Springs sat vulnerably and out in the open. Anyone could sneak in and rob them blind if they let their guard down for any amount of time.

He also needed to come up with a way to make ammunition with limited supplies. Picking up his shell casings, he pocketed them and climbed on his horse. Every little bit would help but the biggest issue was where they would find gunpowder.

Ryan forced a smile. He could bask in the glory for a little while. Eating a good meal would help boost morale, which they desperately needed. "Let's go get these boars cleaned up. We'll be sitting fat and happy in a few hours."

CHAPTER THREE

Darryl didn't have to tell Cecilia that Ryan had gone out on another dangerous escapade. She could tell by the look on his face that his son was up to something, and he didn't want to be the one to tell her. She tried not to be angry – it was in Ryan's nature to be the leader and protect them. She just wasn't sure how much worry she could take. And she feared his luck would soon run out.

"Why the long face, Cecilia?" Her mother reached for her hand, guiding her to the edge of the cot. "Take a load off. You've been pacing for almost an hour now."

Cecilia admired how strong her mother had been through all of this. She had lost her soul mate over all of this, and she appeared to be doing fine – or maybe she was just an excellent actress and was fooling everyone. She wondered if she'd be the woman that Margaret was if something had happened to Ryan. She shuddered to think about it and brushed the thoughts aside. She didn't want to put it out in the open – karma seemed to be getting them a lot lately.

"I just can't sit still. I feel like I should be doing something." Cecilia checked on Ty – he had befriended another boy his age from a family she didn't know. They played in a corner of the shelter, their homemade paper airplanes entertaining them. Seeing him actively playing and laughing eased her nerves. He hadn't skipped a beat with his missing arm. His transition to using only one arm was remarkable.

"You've got something on your mind, and you'll tell me when you're ready," Margaret replied. "You miss your father, don't you?"

"Of course, I do, Mom. I hate that it happened the way it did. And now Ryan is off gallivanting around the area, chasing after dangerous men who wouldn't think twice to take his life. I'm trying to not whine. I'm trying hard to accept all...this." She opened her arms as if she were about to hug someone. "It's like we're in a movie, you know?"

Margaret nodded, her eyes full of wisdom from her seventy-two years of life. "I understand all of the emotions you're feeling."

"How are you so calm? So patient?" Cecilia wondered, her eyes downcast. She was ashamed of her actions toward her husband. She should support Ryan better.

"Years of practice, Cecilia. I didn't get this way overnight."

"Yeah. We're being tested by some higher power. I never got the opportunity to study. I'm going to flunk." Cecilia felt the warmth in the corners of her eyes and the tears welled up, trickling down her cheeks. She laughed, shocking herself at the immediate roller coaster of emotions coursing through her.

"You're handling it a lot better than you think, Cecilia. Don't sell yourself short."

"I'm so happy that Ryan found you. I'm glad that we're all together."

"Me too, hon."

During the day, they had been keeping the upper door to the shelter open. From the sun shining in, Cecilia couldn't tell who was looking in. Standing, she tried to see, her heart skipping a beat when she realized it was Steve. Where was Ryan, and why did he look so surprised? Taking the steps down, he joined them, and Mindy followed. He was so excited that he could barely form a sentence. Cecilia's initial thought was that something had happened to Ryan, and she wanted to reach down his throat to pull the words out of him.

"Ryan killed two wild boars. We'll have a feast tonight!" Steve's breathing was labored, and he gasped to try to control it. "It's about 200 pounds of meat so it should feed us for more than one meal."

"When did y'all decide to go hunting?" Mindy asked.

So that's where they went? Cecilia knew there was an ulterior motive to their escapade. Darryl had been acting too weird around her for it just to be hunting. And if that was what really happened, Darryl would've been chomping at the bit to go with them. He was an excellent shot and was known for his hunting skills.

"That's great about the food!" Cecilia chimed in. "Where is Ryan right now?"

"Cleaning the boars. He and his dad know what they're doing with that, so I backed away. I don't even know where to begin when it comes to stuff like that."

"Will you keep an eye on Ty, Mom?"

Cecilia went up the stairs to ground level, eyes scanning for where her husband and father-in-law might be working. Chief Rayburn didn't have to ask – he knew what she needed and pointed in their direction. They were near the pasture, both hogs laid out on a concrete slab, Ryan on his knees as Darryl directed him.

As she approached, Cecilia cringed when they ripped back the fur, exposing a layer of muscle and fat underneath. Shoving that aside, she tried to imagine how the cooked meat would taste and how it'd help replenish the nutrition deficits they were all suffering from. It was important for Ty – though it had been a few months since his amputation, the child was still recovering from the shock of losing a limb. It'd be very beneficial for his development and growth.

Ryan looked up for a split second, stopping his work as he made eye contact with her, and then continued. His arms were covered in the hog's blood and his jeans were soaked with red. He looked like a starving mountain man with his disheveled hair, beard, and tattered clothes. And despite all of that, she still had a driving force that found him attractive, even in that state. It was their deep-rooted instincts coming out, and though she worried constantly about what he was up to, the fact that he was their protector made her love him even deeper.

"Hey, Cecilia!" Darryl waved, his hands also red-stained from the bloody carcasses.

"Hey. Steve is beside himself about this. I think everyone is."

Ryan nodded as he continued butchering their dinner. He didn't say anything and focused on his task. Darryl crouched beside him, gathering up the fur. It was wiry and probably wouldn't be useful for blankets, but they could use it for something. Cecilia instantly thought about pork rinds, and how it was a snack she used to enjoy with some Tabasco sauce.

"Did you go to hunt or..." She cut herself off. She wasn't going to nag him. She always promised herself that she'd never be a nagging wife. And how could she after he had brought food home for everyone?

"This wasn't our ultimate goal but at least it wasn't a wasted trip." Ryan finally spoke up, handing the knife to his father, who took over. Wiping his hands on the front of his shirt, the red smeared into the fabric, making him look like a sadistic killer. "I didn't tell you. I know you're pissed."

"No, I'm not pissed, Ryan."

"Good. It seems like we've sort of lost ourselves in all of this, you know?" Ryan watched his father work, his eyes downcast. "We haven't had the chance to talk. Or, you know, get to the finer things in life." He wrapped his arm around her waist and pulled her in, his body thinner than she had ever felt it. They had all lost so much weight from food rations that their clothes were barely staying on. She didn't even care that he was likely smearing the hog's blood on her clothing - none of that mattered.

Resting her forehead on his, she shivered when his lips brushed over hers. Cupping the back of his head, her fingers entangled his moist hair, his dark locks sweaty from hours in the sun. The kiss grew deeper, and she tasted the salt on his skin. How she longed to be alone with him – she couldn't remember the last time they had even made love.

"Cut it out, you two!" Ryan pulled away first. Steve and Mindy were walking their way, both laughing as if they were teenagers in middle school. "I'd say get a room, but we're plum out of places to stay!" Steve nudged Ryan who didn't look as amused as their two friends did.

"We're just about done getting them ready," Ryan said, pointing at the piles of pork they'd soon be feasting on.

"Good. We need to get the fire going so we can start our pig roast. I can't wait!" Steve slid his palms together and smacked his lips. "If we had some cold beer to go along with it, now that'd be a good time!"

"We could always make some jailhouse hooch," Ryan exclaimed, a smile finally easing his furrowed brow. "I'm sure Doug knows a few recipes. I don't think he's got a pristine record when it comes to the law."

"All it takes is some bread and some peppermint and we could get something brewing!"

Steve's comment made everyone laugh. It was a nice break from the seriousness of the tribulations going on around them. And for a second, Cecilia's worries were pushed aside.

"Harper Springs is gonna have a nice little shindig tonight!" Steve rejoiced, taking his hat off and throwing it in the air. "Let's get that fire kicked up. I'm starving!"

❄

RYAN, Cecilia, and Ty sat together around the fire. The boars were roasting above the open flame, everyone was circled around it, and everything felt normal. Steve and Mindy were nearby, Margaret was there, and Darryl was helping cook.

The scent of the roasted pork was amazing. Ryan's stomach growled and his mouth watered. He felt like a child, growing impatient as he waited for his food to be ready. The juices dripped into the flames, hissing as the meat slowly turned above. He was almost to the point of calling it done but couldn't risk everyone getting sick off of undercooked meat. With no decent medical treatments, it could become deadly.

"Those pigs are ugly!" Ty pointed as he bounced around. "Daddy, did you kill those pigs?"

"I did, Ty. They are ugly, aren't they?"

"I don't know if I'll like it!"

"When it's ready, take one bite, and I bet you'll eat a ton!" Ryan exclaimed, hugging him. "It's going to taste so much better than those canned weenies you always eat, I promise!"

Cecilia leaned against his shoulder, resting her head on him. She had been quiet. Ryan chalked it up to her being tired. Even though she claimed she wasn't mad at him for all his dangerous plans, he knew better. He knew she was upset but he was trying to keep everyone safe, especially his family. He hoped the looters had decided to move on but with all their progress in Harper Springs had made them a target for those kinds of groups.

And now, they had a raging fire going after dark. It was probably alerting people for miles, making the target over their heads even bigger. But tonight, he had to let it happen. What was the point of everything they had done if they couldn't cut loose and enjoy themselves sometimes? But he also couldn't let his guard down. He had his handgun on him, and it was loaded and ready to go. This would be the perfect time to attack them. And unfortunately, the looters weren't stupid.

Ryan spotted Chief Rayburn on the other side of the fire, standing behind everyone. He had to assume that he was also ready to take action and found comfort in knowing that others were keeping an eye out for their safety. He couldn't carry this all on his own.

Easing to a standing position, Ryan looked down at his family. Ty was focused on the fire, his eyes wide at the marvelous sight in front of them. Most children would snub their nose at the way the food was being cooked but even he was hungry enough to not fight it.

"I'm gonna go talk to Chief for a second," Ryan said, forcing a smile. Cecilia nodded and turned to face the fire again.

Approaching his superior, Ryan leaned back against a tree and folded his arms over his chest. Neither man spoke at first, both listening to the crackling of the dry wood being devoured by the hot flames. The majority were orange, but deep inside the fire, green and blue flames licked the lower pieces of wood. Fire had always fascinated Ryan which was a huge reason he joined the volunteer fire department. Tonight, it was mesmerizing, almost having a hypnotizing effect on him.

"How's your son doing?" Chief Rayburn asked.

"He acts like it never even happened," Ryan replied. "He's resilient. Almost makes me jealous at how fast he's adapted but I'm glad he's doing so well. It's just so hard to believe all of this is still happening. Hell, that it ever happened in the first place."

"It was bound to happen."

"What do you mean?" Ryan inquired, finally able to pull his gaze away from the fire and face Chief.

"It's science, Ryan. All this man-made stuff certainly must play a factor in the way the atmosphere is. All the pollution from cars, the pollution in general."

"I don't know, Chief. Something seems off. I get the whole global warming debacle. I'm not sure what I believe and don't believe about it. This is all an eye-opener for me. It's just odd, that's all. I've never been a scientist, but I've always been fascinated with the weather. This has me baffled."

Chief Rayburn smiled and pointed toward the roasting boars.

"Good job on the hunting today. You're definitely the favorite around these parts right now."

It was a quick change of subject and Ryan noticed a shift in Chief Rayburn's demeanor. He seemed quieter than usual, staying in the shadows when decisions needed to be made. The Chief Rayburn he remembered was front and center, ready to help, direct, and get the job done. Lately, Ryan felt like he had slid into that role. Maybe it was everyone – even Cecilia was acting differently. He couldn't fault them. Adjusting to the new way of life was complicated. It was hard accepting that this was the new normal after being so spoiled with the technology they had just months before.

"Everyone come get some! It's time to eat!" Steve yelled over the roar of the fire, and everyone formed a line around the slab where they laid the meat out.

Ryan rejoined Cecilia and Ty, helping his son load his plate with meat. There wasn't much else to go with it since the vegetables hadn't produced anything yet but no one seemed to cared. It was a hearty meal that was much better than the processed junk they had been eating.

Ryan bit into a piece and the first bite was like heaven. The outer skin was flaky like a pork rind, and he had to remind himself to go slow. It had been long enough that if they ate too much at once, they could make themselves sick from their bodies not being used to such a rich entree. Everything fell silent as everyone ate. The fire was dying down some which was good – it was still very hot out despite the sun going down.

"This is so good, Daddy!" Ty finished the last bite on his plate and wiped his mouth with the back of his arm.

"It is, isn't it?"

"Good job on the hunt," Cecilia said, nibbling on hers.

"That was the easy part."

"Yeah?"

"Yeah. The hard part is finding a way to preserve all of this. It'd be a shame if it all went to waste."

Ryan knew the two boars would be more than enough to feed everyone. With food rationing, everyone was used to eating a much lesser amount of food for a meal, which also meant their stomachs had shrunk. It was a good supply to keep around and use as needed – without refrigerators or freezers, they'd have to think of a way to keep it safe. The fact that it was pork made it even more important that they prevented food born illness and the growth of salmonella and botulism. Not to mention that pork was known for tapeworms.

"Enjoy your meal, Ryan." Cecilia nudged his arm. "Stop worrying about everything, even if it's just for a few minutes. Do that for me, okay?"

"I can try. No promises, though."

It would be nice to be able to stop worrying, like an on-and-off switch in his brain. He'd have to pretend he wasn't ruminating about everything. If it meant easing the tension with Cecilia, he'd put up a front. Deep down, Ryan's mind was racing a mile a minute.

CHAPTER FOUR

Insomnia was something Ryan was used to. His body begged for him to stay in bed, and though he was both physically and mentally exhausted, he couldn't get his brain to shut down long enough to catch some sleep. The storm cellar was pitch black. He could hear the deep breathing of those around him, the occasional snore breaking the white noise of the synchronized breaths.

He had enjoyed his time by Cecilia's side, but he was antsy. The immediate threat of the looters attacking prompted the townspeople to come up with a plan to hold watch. Some of the firefighters and other men of Harper Springs had taken turns, patrolling the perimeter of their new city limits. With only one man at a time doing it, they were probably not watching as well as they should, and it was better than nothing. It was Ryan's night off and yet he still couldn't get a full night's sleep. Except for the night before, when Steve and Cecilia claimed he had slept like a rock, the one hour of rest here and there was as good as it was going to get.

Kicking his legs off the side of the cot, Ryan slipped into his jeans and padded toward the stairs. There was a lantern lit in a far corner, providing just enough light to see where he was going.

They had to put rations on the propane – during the day they only ran a few and if people needed light, they had to go to ground level. Occasionally they'd leave the shelter door open. It was letting the cooler air out, hindering any chance of a reprieve from the high temperatures.

When Ryan got to ground level, there was a slight chill in the air that caught him off guard. It was a nice change to not feel the sweltering heat, even at night. He could smell the air transitioning to autumn – it was a little earlier than usual for the area but something he wasn't going to complain about. The biggest issue of an early fall would be the vegetation – due to the late planting, they were late developing, which meant a late harvest. Hopefully, their first freeze would be late too, and it would just stay cool.

He couldn't recall whose turn it was to take watch. He felt the weight of his gun in his pocket, feeling a little better that it was with him. It was shocking how much things had changed – he had taken two lives through everything, and though the guilt still tore at him, he wouldn't hesitate to do it again if it meant their safety was compromised. He often wondered how he'd handle an intruder or threat to his family – it was situational speculation that a person would only know how they'd react if it was happening. Now Ryan knew – he'd kill to protect the ones he cared about.

"What are you doing out here? It's your night off, Gibson." Chief Rayburn approached him, the moon illuminating his face.

"Couldn't sleep."

"Sounds about like me. I'm sure you'll be glad to hear that I haven't seen a damn thing. No one has since we've been doing this."

Both men walked toward the hill that overlooked their pasture. Sitting, Ryan stretched his legs out in front of him and looked out over the town. Small structures were being built – an area to clean their kills from hunting, a place to store their farm equipment, and people had started talking about rebuilding homes. Lumber was the biggest setback – they could gather from trees, but the buildings wouldn't be as strong as before. The majority of businesses and houses were brick before the tornadoes came in and destroyed everything.

"What's on your mind, Ryan?"

"It'd be a shorter conversation if I told you what I wasn't worried about. What do you think about building a fence around the town?"

Chief Rayburn looked up at the sky and over to Ryan, glancing at him from the corner of his eye. "I've thought about it. Depending on how tall we were to do it, it'd be a good added piece of protection. If someone wants to come into our town bad enough, they'd clear it, but it would make their life a little more difficult in the process."

"Yeah. No telling how much wood it'd take. And nails." Ryan groaned out in frustration. "Back during the good times, you get an idea, run to the hardware store, and go with it. Even after all these months, it's still a hard habit to break. Kind of like when the electricity would go out and you'd still reach for the light switch even though you *knew* it was out!"

Chief Rayburn laughed. "That's a good way to put it, Ryan. My basement served as my storage room back at my place. We were able to scrounge up a lot of items that will be useful if we do build a wall. Several hammers, drawers full of nails and screws, even some rolls of barbed wire I was about to start putting up on my farm."

"That's the best news I've heard in a long time. Ranks right up there with the feast we had tonight."

"When the sun comes up, we can take an inventory of what we have. We'll have to go chop some more trees down. With the lack of rain and the damage already done to them, it shouldn't be hard to do it."

Ryan took a deep breath and looked up at the sky. There were no clouds, and the blanket of stars was breathtaking. With no streetlights to hinder the view, it was possibly the prettiest sight he had seen in a long time. Taking a moment to appreciate nature was a nice change of pace instead of cursing it.

"I want answers, Chief. I want to know why this is happening, how widespread it is, and what we can do to get it to stop."

"I wouldn't want to dig too deep, Ryan. Sometimes we come up with answers we might not want to know about."

"What do you mean?" Ryan asked, pulling his concentration from the beautiful night sky.

"Sometimes ignorance is bliss. Do you understand, Gibson?"

"I get it, but I guess not for this situation. You don't want to know how to get it to stop?"

Chief Rayburn ducked his head and ran his fingers through the sand beneath them. His shoulders slumped like he was carrying a thousand pounds. It wasn't the usual confident Chief that Ryan worked with.

"We haven't had anything extreme happen lately, have we? I think it is finally dying down."

Ryan shook his head and scoffed. He tried not to get riled up but it was attitudes like his Chief's that would set them back. "You don't consider multiple months in a row at one hundred plus degrees temperatures as extreme? You don't consider that same amount of time going by with absolutely no form of precipitation falling from the sky? I get it, we aren't Seattle. We don't get rain every day but even this is unheard of."

"We've had some bad droughts. We aren't where the dust bowl took place, but we are close. History repeats itself, even with the weather."

"I don't know, Chief. Even back then, they were able to get out and get to safety. We have advanced technology and ways of getting news to others and still nothing. Where is FEMA? Where is Red Cross? Just by the way the air smells and feels tonight, winter will be coming early. Spring and summer were out of control. What if winter follows suit? And I have a feeling it will."

"It's a little early to be making those kinds of predictions."

"I predicted the drought, and I was right," Ryan replied, grabbing a fist full of dirt. Watching it trickle between his fingers, a gust of wind carried some of it off.

Chief Rayburn lowered his voice, almost too low to be heard over the wind. "I think we shouldn't pry. I don't think it'll solve a damn thing. We should just accept this as a new normal, rebuild, and get on with our lives."

"I can't do that, Chief," Ryan said, standing. "We put a man on the moon. We have the internet that allows getting news out there fast. We have advanced weather forecasting to give people good warning to take cover in events like these." He patted some dust from his jeans and took a few steps before turning back around. "I guess I should be using past-tense. We *had* all those things. Now we're nothing better than cavemen. I can't help that my curiosity is running rampant. Something is off and no, ignorance isn't bliss. I want it to stop. I want this country to reunite so we can work together as a team. This *can't* be how life is from now on. I'm not gonna let that be the solution."

"I wouldn't get your hopes up too high, Ryan. I think this is well beyond anything we can comprehend."

Ryan ignored Chief Rayburn's last comment and strode back down the hill toward the shelter. He never was the type to roll over and die. He thought Chief Rayburn wasn't either but if there was one thing for certain in all of this, it was that people's true colors were beginning to show. Ryan wasn't going to let himself fall into the darkness of giving up. He didn't want that kind of future for Ty or his family.

❄

RYAN GOT out of bed the next morning and began working. Staying busy, he watered the crops and helped gather supplies to start building a wall around Harper Springs. He kept his focus on a possible attack. The looters still had not come back around and each day that went by without a sighting, Ryan worried more. He feared complacency the most, worrying he'd be one of the first to fall into a rut of thinking they were safe from any kind of attack. That's just what the nuisances wanted – just when they thought they were the supreme new town with the biggest driving force, they'd catch them on their heels and take over with no problem.

Gun supply wasn't a problem – if they wanted to keep hunting to replenish their food, it would mean using up their ammunition. There were ways to make homemade bullets. It consisted of gathering the right supplies to do it – metal being the most important thing. Ryan could sift through debris piles to do just that. He'd also need a melting pot, a consistent source of heat to melt the metal, and a bullet mold, which his father had from his years of recycling his own ammunition. That was another chance of fate that had worked in their favor.

He saw Steve from atop the hill and joined him. It was still a little before dawn and the heat of the day hadn't kicked in. It was probably cool enough for a jacket, but Ryan was enjoying it. He'd never again complain about cool weather after the summer they had endured.

"Morning, Steve."

"Morning, Ryan. From the looks of things, you didn't sleep a wink last night, did you?"

"Not a one. But I've gotten a lot done this morning. And good news – looks like a few of the plants are starting to produce. Nothing is ready to be picked but hey, it's progress."

"That's great!"

Ryan glanced over at the charred ground where they had their bonfire and meal the night before. They had put the remaining meat in a box with a lid on it. Since the meat had been smoked, the fear of food contamination had been reduced, but Ryan still wanted to make sure they stored it properly.

Lifting the box, Steve helped him carry it to the basement where a business used to stand. It wasn't safe enough for many people to go in – the ladder at the entrance was compromised and rickety, and whoever used it had to take it slow. The wood was weak under Ryan's boots, and he made a mental note to add repairing it to his ever-growing to-do list.

The walls and floor were dirt, and he was able to dig a deep hole in the side. The musty scent stung his nostrils. It was damp and cool, and would serve as their refrigerator. Sliding the box inside, he wiped his hands on his shirt and studied the remaining room they had to work with.

"We cooked all the meat, right?"

"Yeah. And by how heavy that box is, I'd say we still have a good fifty to seventy-five pounds. You think it's cool enough in here to keep it safe?"

"Yeah. Smoking is a good way to preserve meat. If we're able to hunt anything else in bulk, we'll need to salt-cure it or find out other means of keeping it fresh. This is how they did it way back when. I remember going to that old ranching heritage museum where they had a storage cellar like this. It's dark and out of sunlight and the air doesn't move too much. It'll help."

"Is it me, or does it feel like the days are starting off a lot cooler?" Steve inquired, climbing back up the ladder. Ryan followed, reaching the top. The sun was now completely up, and it was a chilly, autumn morning.

"Yeah, it has been. I'd say it's only in the upper fifties right now. Usually, by now, it's at least ninety. The chill of an early fall, Steve. You know what that means – we're probably going to have an El Nino winter."

"I'm from Oklahoma. We are used to having more of a winter than y'all do down here."

"And it's not such a bad thing. If it snows a lot or we get ice storms, it's precipitation and I'm at the point where I'll welcome any kind. The river is low, and I haven't been down to the lake lately to check, but it doesn't take a genius to figure out it'll be the same story down there."

Ryan watched Chief Rayburn walk past them. He didn't acknowledge them, like he was lost in his own world. He couldn't shake the conversation he had with him the night before. It only heightened his insomnia, making his worry spiral out of control. Chief was changing – the tragedy likely hitting him harder than Ryan had realized.

"Hey, Steve, can I ask you something?"

"Sure."

"Are you the type that wants to find out why something is happening, or would you rather just not want to know?"

Steve contemplated the question, pursing his lips. "Depends on what it's about."

"All of this." Ryan spread his hands and turned in a circle. "Why has Mother Nature gone completely psycho on us? And why are we so crippled with all the advances we've made in technology and weather forecasting?"

"Yeah. I'd like to figure it out. I just don't know how to go about doing it."

"Me neither," Ryan replied, keeping his eye on Chief Rayburn. He appeared busy but wasn't doing much of anything. "All I know is winter is coming fast. If the pattern continues, we're going to freeze to death."

Chief Rayburn approached them, and the man Ryan once trusted to lead them into fires and direct them on emergency calls had transitioned to a man that Ryan probably wouldn't take orders from. It was a shame – Chief was always cool under pressure.

"You still inquiring about what is going on around here?"

"Yeah, I am, Mike," Ryan replied, choosing a bold move to use Chief's first name, an informal salutation that he never did before.

"Mike?" Chief asked, cocking his head to the side. "We're on a first-name basis now?"

"The way I see it, with whatever the hell is happening here, in times of a tragedy as huge as this, we're all on an even playing field. There's no such thing as rank anymore. You are Mike Rayburn. I am Ryan Gibson. This is Steve Tarrant. We're all working together as one, aren't we?"

"Yes, we are, though going on a wild goose chase to find out why is only going to put your energy on a lost cause."

Ryan nodded and clicked his tongue. His wanting to get answers apparently struck a nerve with Rayburn. "I guess you can say that curiosity killed the cat."

"In this instance, satisfaction won't bring it back." Mike took a step toward Ryan, prodding his index finger into Ryan's chest.

"I disagree, Mike." Ryan made sure his tone was sarcastic when he said his name. "I gotta get busy building the wall. I might be heading out on another mission soon." He was bluffing, but getting a rise out of Rayburn was about the only satisfaction he felt lately. Either Chief didn't like not calling the shots or there was something deeper going on with him.

Ryan was far too mentally exhausted to figure it out. But soon, he'd get around to digging deeper. If it meant getting their life back to normal, he'd be willing to do anything possible to make a good future for Ty, Cecilia, and the rest of the people he had grown to care so much about. This wasn't just a normal nature cycle. It was beyond what an average, everyday Joe could comprehend, and Ryan wouldn't give up on getting the answers they needed to stabilize the situation.

"Ryan, Hon, come grab some breakfast! Ty wants you to have some oatmeal with him!" Cecilia stuck her head out of the shelter, waving for him to join them.

"I'll be right there. Steve, come grab a bite. We've got a busy day ahead of us."

CHAPTER FIVE

Cecilia gathered up her family's large pile of dirty clothes from their corner of the shelter. With Ty becoming more active, he was doing a great job of getting his pants and shirts soiled. She enjoyed seeing him making friends with some of the other kids – there weren't that many around to begin with and his socializing was a major factor in his recovery. The more fresh air and exercise he got, the better his body would respond to everything they were going through.

Playing also meant burning calories. They were already malnourished and not getting enough nutrients to replace what they were spending. She noticed everyone's clothes fitting more loosely. If she could come across some of Mrs. McElroy's sewing stuff, she could bring in the waistbands to help adjust to their dwindling sizes. It was worrisome – she was always a thin woman but now, if she had gone into a department store and sized a pair of jeans, she'd likely be a size two or smaller.

The same was true for Ryan. He was never a chubby man, but he had bulk from muscle. He was still lean but thinning down. Working from sun up to sun down had helped aid in staying muscled but he was also facing the issue of more caloric burn than caloric intake. She saw it mainly in his face, especially after he shaved his beard. He had been keeping some facial hair to protect his skin from the sun, but it was shocking to see her family wasting away before her eyes.

Carrying the dirty laundry in a pillowcase, she headed to the river where she gathered some water in a bucket. She didn't want to clean the clothes in their source of drinking water, though it didn't take a wise person to realize that it was possibly getting contaminated by other things. At least she was doing her part in attempting to keep it clean.

Cecilia could fit several articles of Ty's clothing in the bucket. Dipping them in and out, she scrubbed the fabric together. His jeans and shirts were getting worn out, the fibers weak from wear and tear. She wished she was better at sewing. Her mom had tried to teach her when she was younger, but she never took a liking to it and never cared to attempt to do it.

The only soap they had was some hand soap that the doctor's office had stockpiled. It wasn't the best for clothes but at least it was something, and she squeezed a few drops in the water, lathering it up as best as she could. The water was turning brown from just Ty's clothes alone but water preservation was important. Ryan wasn't too particular about his clothing – it'd take him a matter of seconds to dirty them up from work anyway.

Margaret had made a laundry line between two trees for them to hand dry their clothes. Cecilia draped their jeans, shirts, and bedding across it, humming as she worked. For the first time in days, it was comfortable to be outside. Was she just getting used to it? With heat as terrible as they had been enduring, there would be no chance that a person could adjust to feeling like they were being baked in an oven.

"Busy at work, huh?"

The comment pulled Cecilia from her daydream, and she looked up, spotting Doug at a distance. It made her heart skip a beat and she almost turned to go the other way.

"You try doing laundry for two boys."

Doug laughed and approached her. "Especially Ryan. Can't get that man to sit still."

"No." Cecilia shook her head and draped his last pair of jeans on the line. She didn't know Doug, didn't trust him, and though Ryan had made amends with him, she still wasn't sure what his agenda was.

"How are you holding up?" He was close enough now to reach out and touch her, but he kept his hands to himself, a genuine look of concern on his face.

"I'm managing." Cecilia didn't mean to be so cold but being alone with him made her nervous. Glancing over her shoulder, she hoped someone was nearby.

"I know you don't like me, Cecilia. I get it. I just wanted to tell you how much I appreciate everything your family has done for me. Ryan and I started on the wrong foot. But if that didn't happen, there's no telling where I'd be right now. Probably dead." He rubbed the back of his neck and smiled. "Though I'm not sure that's such a bad thing."

"What do you mean?" Cecilia asked.

"We're just... you know..."

"Just what?" Cecilia had an idea where he was taking the conversation, but she wanted him to say it.

"Nothing. Never mind. It's not important." He walked past her toward town and turned on his heel, facing her again. "Will you tell Ryan thanks for me? I'm not too good at sentiments and I don't think he is either. Coming from you, I think it'll carry more weight."

"Sure, Doug, I'll tell him. Are you going somewhere?"

"Going somewhere?" Doug arched his eyebrow.

"It just seems like a goodbye is all."

Doug smiled but didn't respond, walking through some brush that crunched under his shoes. Cecilia's pulse raced and the hair on the back of her neck stood up. The vibe in the air felt off and something deep inside was telling her to get back to the shelter around everyone else. It was like she was being watched from a distance. Or maybe it was just her imagination – if so, it was powerful enough to freak her out.

She'd come back for their clothes. It'd take them a while to dry, and others had left there's unattended. Hurrying back up the hill, she tried to regain her composure before everyone saw her. Doug was nowhere to be found, vanishing after his odd request.

Ty was playing with a couple of other children, her mother keeping an eye on him. Ryan and Steve were piling up wood for some new project that they had thought up. Everything was normal. She could take a breath and calm down. It was a simple freak-out that almost turned into a full-blown panic attack.

"You get the laundry hung up?" Margaret asked, handing her some water.

"I did."

"Take a load off. You look exhausted, dear. Did you run back? You're out of breath!"

"I'm fine, Mom. You're right, I'm just tired." Sipping the water, she downed it fast and checked on Ty. Was someone watching her? Or was she just paranoid due to Ryan's speculation of the looters?

❄

CECILIA'S BROW creased as she looked up at the sky. "I don't know. It was just strange is all."

Ryan sat beside her, patting her knee. He had a brilliant idea to have her join him at dusk to watch the sunset. She had to see the stars – hopefully, they would look just as magnificent as the night before.

"What did he say, exactly?" Ryan laid back on the blanket, easing Cecilia down beside him. The cool night air felt great, and he tried not to harp on the possibility of an early winter shifting to a complete reality.

"He said to tell you thank you for everything you've done."

"He's told me that multiple times. I wonder why he'd tell you as well unless he was needing an icebreaker to get you in his good graces too."

"No. It felt like a goodbye," Cecilia replied, turning on her side, resting on her elbow. Reaching out, she skimmed her hand down the side of Ryan's face, feeling the sandpaper facial hair she was starting to get used to. His tanned skin was darker than normal, the sun taking its toll on him.

"A goodbye? You think he's running off?"

"You think he could be rejoining the looters?" Cecilia's eyes widened and she rolled back over onto her back.

"I sure hope not. That could be bad for us." Ryan clasped his hands behind his head. Never a dull moment! If Doug decided to go back to the looters, he'd have perfect intel to give them about how they were doing things. Food supply, locations of supplies, their foreseeable plans of town progression. Ryan gritted his teeth at the thought of it. It took a lot for him to gain the trust of someone. And only seconds of assumption for him to lose it.

"What else could he be up to?"

Ryan shrugged and stretched his legs out. A beer would've been perfect to ease his nerves. Maybe he should start making jailhouse hooch. It'd be great to drink when someone needed an escape.

"I'd like to think he was just being sincere. That's what I have to tell myself right now. If I add just another ounce of worry onto everything, my head might explode."

"I don't know." Cecilia shrugged and leaned against him. "Feels like a red flag to me."

"I'll have my dad talk to him. They seemed to bond well when they were going to Fox Lake."

"I've just had a weird feeling altogether. When I was hanging laundry, I could've sworn someone was watching me. And the stuff with Doug. Is there a full moon tonight because it's like the crazies are coming out?"

Ryan looked up at the moon, admiring the silver silhouette shining off it. It wasn't a full moon but it was big and bright, lighting up the pasture in front of them. He had a good feeling about their crops. They'd likely not produce huge vegetables starting off, but it was a building process and it meant progress.

They both sat in silence for a while, Ryan enjoying the feel of the rise and fall of Cecilia's breathing. Coyotes howled in the distance, sounding oddly like a far-off woman screaming into the night air. He remembered thinking that's what it was when he was a kid. There were too many ghost stories involving wolves howling at the moon. Only tonight, it was real life and those wild packs of dogs were hungry and looking for food.

After another hour alone, both Cecilia and Ryan agreed to head back to the shelter. They wanted to check on Ty and their family. Ryan also wanted to see if Doug was around. Though he swore to himself that he wasn't going to obsess over it, his biggest concern was whether he was going to betray them and go back to the looters. With everything he knew, it would give the criminals the upper hand if it did come down to war.

Everyone was turning in for the night with several lanterns across the room fading. Ryan heaved a sigh of relief when he spotted Doug lying on his cot, his eyes closed. From his tense body language, the man wasn't asleep, but Ryan thought it best to leave him be. If the opportunity allowed him, he'd speak with him in the morning.

"Ryan, don't forget you have the first watch tonight." Chief Rayburn patted him on the arm, acting as if their heated exchange of words hadn't happened. Ryan nodded in acknowledgment but was caught so far off guard that he didn't know how to respond.

He checked on Ty who was busy coloring with a lava rock he had found outside. Swirling the black around on a piece of paper, he glanced up and smiled at Ryan, and focused back on his work. Margaret seemed to be doing okay, sliding under a wool blanket and Darryl was brushing his teeth. Everyone was accounted for and ready for bed. Ryan should've felt confident to leave them for his turn to watch. But something still nagged at him.

Joining his father, Ryan handed him a towel. "You talk to Doug recently?" He kept his voice low. He didn't want to admit it, but Ryan was developing a trust issue with a lot of people, including everyone he knew from days before the tragedy.

"Just in passing. Why?"

"Just something he said to Cecilia. We need to keep an eye on him."

"What did he say?" Darryl wiped a glob of toothpaste from the corner of his mouth.

Looking around the room, Ryan guided his father away from everyone. Paranoia was never something he enjoyed feeling but right now, if he were put in front of a psychologist, they'd say he was certifiable.

"It's not so much *what* he said... more like *how* he said it, Dad."

"You're not making any sense, Ryan."

"He thanked Cecilia for everything we've done for him." Saying it out loud did sound ridiculous. Maybe it was a mistake bringing his father into it.

"And?" Darryl arched his eyebrow and draped the towel over his shoulder.

"Like I said... how he said it. Cecilia said it seemed like he was telling her goodbye."

"Goodbye? Where the hell would he go?" Darryl's voice rose and Ryan cringed, putting his index finger to his lips to remind his father to keep his voice low.

"I don't know. Possibly stabbing us in the back to help the looters?"

"Nah. I don't think so."

"How well do we know him?" Ryan asked, glancing over his shoulder. Doug was still on his cot, his body more relaxed as he had finally fallen asleep.

"I guess not well but I would hate to think that. Emotions are running high right now, Ryan. What if he was just truly being sincere and Cecilia misconstrued it? She doesn't know him at all. How would she know what he truly meant?"

"I don't know." Ryan sighed and raked his hand through his hair. "Maybe I'm just over-analyzing it, but I'd hate for him to run off on us. He'd be an excellent source for the looters."

"He would but I think you're reading way too much into it."

"Maybe." Ryan wasn't convinced. Something still nagged at him that there was something off. Maybe it wasn't Doug possibly running away. There was something not quite right with Doug and the impression he gave Cecilia. "Listen, I gotta get up to ground level. It's my turn to pull watch duty."

"Be careful, Son. I'll keep an eye on everyone. And relax. You're letting your mind play tricks on you."

Ryan took the stairs two at a time and checked his handgun. The magazine was fully loaded and ready to go. With help from the moon, he was getting a nice view over Harper Springs. Sitting in the same spot he and Cecilia had recently been at, his eyes scanned in every direction – north, east, south, and west. It was a clear night, and the temperatures were cool. The smell of fall surrounded Ryan and he took it in.

He tried to think the best of people. He'd be more than happy to be wrong about his and Cecilia's assumptions about Doug. He had to stop worrying about it eventually but now wasn't the time. The fact that Doug was down in the shelter close to his family made his skin crawl. What in the hell was that man up to?

CHAPTER SIX

Ryan finished his watch and instead of going back to the shelter after Steve took over, he took a walk. Being mindful of his surroundings, he walked along the probable fence line they were going to put up around the perimeter of Harper Springs. He hadn't seen any movement the whole time he took watch, but he was just one man and there were four directions anyone could come in from – or leave from, which made him think about Doug.

If Doug did leave to turn against them, Ryan would have to speed up the process of making more ammunition. He'd love it if he could make guns as well but that was asking for too much supply that they didn't have. It was like they had to develop their own military simply to keep intruders out. Since the American government had completely forgotten about them, or possibly even crippled themselves, it was every man for themselves. Ryan just hoped that in battle everyone would stick together.

Walking the outer edge of town was calming. He made sure to let Steve know of his plans so the other guy wouldn't see him in the distance and alert everyone. To be hurt or killed by friendly fire would be a tragedy after everything they had accomplished.

Building the fence was going to take a lot. The temperatures were starting to cooperate, though transitioning quicker than what was normal. Ryan looked up at the night sky, admiring the same blanket of stars he had with Cecilia – the view was spectacular, lending a silver silhouette up against the outline of the top of the mountains. It was like a panoramic picture a professional photographer would take.

He padded past the roped horse corrals, the temporary storage area they had concocted, and back to the shelter. Sleep was still his enemy, and he wanted to check on everything, especially on Doug. If he was within view of someone Ryan trusted, his worries of treason would dissipate.

The door to the cellar squeaked open and Ryan tried to stay as quiet as possible. It was pitch dark except for a lamp near the bathroom area. He grabbed a flashlight and waited until he was closer to where Doug was sleeping before turning it on. Cecilia, Ty, Margaret, and Darryl were safe on their cots, snoozing away. Ryan envied their capability to sleep so well. Maybe he'd eventually get there.

Weaving around others, he clicked the flashlight on, making sure to not flash the beam directly on Doug. His heart skipped a beat when he saw the empty cot – the blanket was kicked back and balled up on the end and Doug's backpack that was usually stored underneath was missing.

"Son of a..." Ryan whispered. The son of a bitch was really doing it! He was turning his back on Harper Springs and the people who were gracious enough to give him a second chance. It was the dead of night. What if he was just overreacting and he woke everyone up over nothing? That wouldn't be wise, and he didn't want to evoke panic on people who were already walking on eggshells.

Ryan hurried back to Steve, running once he got to ground level. His lungs burned and his body ached, begging for him to sit down and rest. His mind played against his body's desires, and he sped up the hill, Steve's eyes widened as he approached him.

"You see anyone leave?" Ryan asked.

"No. It's been dead."

"I can't believe this shit!" Ryan rested his hand on the top of his head and looked around. "That's the last time I ever trust someone I don't know!"

"What in the hell is going on, Ryan?" Steve stood up and touched Ryan's shoulder, making him stop moving in a circle.

"Doug is gone."

"Gone? Where?"

"I don't know."

"You're going to have to explain, Ryan. I didn't realize we were running a prison here. People are free to come and go as they please, right?"

"Of course," Ryan replied, pacing. "But Doug used to be one of them." Ryan motioned his hand outward toward the empty pastures and fields where he was certain many of the looters were hiding and watching. "Cecilia talked to him earlier. She said he was acting weird like he was saying goodbye. Considering his history, my first assumption is he left to rejoin the looters."

"That's his choice, Ryan. If he is doing that, let the son of a bitch go!"

"It's not that easy," Ryan said, shaking his head. "He knows our plans. All that shit. He knows where we keep our supplies. It's like having a spy. And it pisses me off!"

Before Ryan could say anything else, Steve patted his chest and pointed to the west toward the mountain range. "Could that be our friend?"

Ryan stepped forward, squinting his eyes. The person walking was at least half a mile away, but it looked like Doug.

"It doesn't matter who it is. We still need to check it out."

Ryan and Steve hurried down the hill, both running full speed toward the mysterious person in the distance. Ryan ignored his body's warnings to stop. He was running on pure adrenaline and if it happened to be Doug deserting them, he wasn't sure what he was going to do. They reached him quickly and when the man turned to face them, it took Ryan's breath away when he confirmed that it was Doug.

"Where in the hell do you think you're going?" Ryan asked, his voice raspy as he gulped to try and catch his breath.

Doug didn't respond. He held a cold and vacant expression and continued to walk as if Ryan and Steve weren't there. Hoisting his backpack, he adjusted it and ducked his head as if he were out for a nice Sunday afternoon stroll.

Ryan glanced at Steve who shrugged. It was weird and again, Ryan asked, "Where are you going, Doug?"

"This doesn't concern you." Finally, Doug spoke, though he didn't look at them.

"I think it does."

"How do you figure?" Doug asked, finally looking at Ryan.

"If you're going back to the looters, it concerns me. It concerns all of us, Doug! It's the safety of my family and friends."

Doug smirked and quickened his pace, getting a few feet ahead of them. "I wouldn't worry about it, Ryan. You worry too damn much."

"We are here for you, buddy," Steve finally chimed in. "Look at all the progress we've made! Why leave now?"

"I meant it when I told your wife thanks for everything y'all have done." Doug hopped on a nearby rise in the ground, standing a few feet taller then Ryan and Doug. His eyes were dark and sunken in, and the once talkative man Ryan had thought he got to know was solemn. "Y'all are good people."

"Then why are you leaving?" Ryan asked. "Like Steve said, we're making progress. Did you see the pasture? We'll be harvesting some vegetables and cotton soon."

"It's all a lost cause. Like I said several times, Ryan. It's just prolonging the inevitable. It's dying slow. And I'm not going to let that happen to me."

Ryan saw the silver in Doug's hand reflect off the moonlight. He tried to dive toward him to stop whatever his plan was. Everything felt like slow motion, but it was too late - the gunshot rang out, its deafening blow echoing against the foothills and mountains behind them.

❄

DARRYL JOLTED UPWARD, sitting up on his cot. He felt the springs bounce beneath him, his breath labored, his heart racing as he tried to gain his composure. Looking around the room, it took him a second to realize where he was. Even after all the months that had passed, he still wasn't used to sleeping in a large room with people he didn't know.

It was dark but he rubbed his eyes to try and get a better view around him. Ryan's cot was empty. Was he still on watch? They were only making each guy stay out a few hours. Steve's cot was empty too. Something felt off and he gathered up his jeans and shirt, slipping into them in hopes of not waking Cecilia. He didn't want to have to explain his concern to her. There was no need to panic. It could've just been a bad dream trickling over into real life. Chances were that Steve and Ryan were just out working in the cool of the night.

Darryl couldn't fight the nagging feeling, and as he walked through all the cots, it heightened when he saw that Doug's cot was also vacant. He thought he had developed enough trust in Doug to not question his every move but the fact that all three of them were gone at the same time wasn't a good thing. He had learned to completely trust his instincts, and something was off.

Checking Cecilia and Ty one more time, he felt comfortable leaving them. They were sound asleep, and it was best if Cecilia was oblivious to whatever might be happening. The woman was already bouncing off the walls with all her worries. There was no need to panic about something Darryl had no clue about yet.

Putting on his jeans and a shirt, Darryl crept up the stairs and outside, the night chill catching him off guard. He had no idea where to go so he headed toward the pasture first. That was where Ryan always went when he had something on his mind.

Reaching the top of the hill, Darryl looked out over the area. The bright moon was helpful and at first, he didn't see a thing. He didn't want to yell out their names in case they were in danger. Ryan had voiced how dangerous the group of looters could be. What if they had kidnapped the three men? Knowing how valuable Ryan and Steve were to Harper Springs, it would've been a bold move that spoke volumes.

Darryl saw movement to the west. Was it Steve and Ryan? He couldn't tell who they were, but it was two men. In his older age, he couldn't run like he used to but what he saw in the distance made Darryl move faster than he had in years, almost as fast as when they got surrounded by the wildfire that almost took their lives.

He was chancing fate, running toward the unknown. He could be stumbling right into a trap and the looters would have four men from Harper Springs. He slowed his pace as he got closer, gasping to get his breathing under control. Ever since the dust storms, Darryl's respiratory issues never got back to normal. He was okay to continue to work but there was a difference in the tightness in his chest. It didn't take a doctor to make him realize that he probably had a mild form of Brown Lung Syndrome.

As he got closer, the scene revealed Ryan kneeling next to a motionless body and Steve standing over him, his hat off, both heads ducked as they looked down. What had happened? Was Ryan forced to take another life out of self-defense?

Both men must have heard him approach because they looked in Darryl's direction, Ryan's eyes widening as he spotted his father. Darryl stopped walking and stood still, his hands raised to his shoulders, making sure Ryan wasn't jumpy.

"What is going on?" Darryl asked, unable to get a look at the person's face. By process of elimination, it was clear the body was Doug. He just wanted to know how the hell it happened.

"It's Doug..." Steve confirmed, his voice trailing off.

"What happened?" Darryl asked, keeping his voice low.

Ryan was sensitive when it came to the two men he had killed so he approached it delicately. Finally taking a few steps forward, he got a better vantage point. Doug's fingers were still wrapped around the handle of the gun, his index finger resting on the trigger. Blood splatter painted the rocks behind him red and he lay in a puddle of his bodily fluids. Though there was no denying he was dead, his eyes stared up at the sky, the blue of his irises bright against his lifeless face.

"I... uh..." Ryan muttered, pushing himself up to a standing position.

"Suicide..." Darryl trailed off, shaking his head. "I don't even know what to say."

Ryan pulled the gun from Doug's hand and emptied the chamber. It was just a six-shooter, so five bullets fell out into his palm.

"He has a bag," Darryl pointed beside his body. "Why would he have that with him if he knew he was about to kill himself?" People did strange things when they were desperate. Maybe his initial plan wasn't suicide. Maybe he just wanted to run away.

Ryan picked it up and unzipped it, sifting through the items inside. A notepad and pen fell out along with a bottle of water, a can of Spam, and two boxes of bullets. Darryl couldn't tell what caliber they were, but it didn't matter. They'd come in handy.

Ryan flipped the notepad open, his eyes skimming over something jotted down on the paper. He didn't say anything but flipped it shut and handed it to Steve. Taking a few steps back, he turned and walked away from the scene. Darryl was curious to see what it said but he'd wait his turn. Steve finished and gave it to him.

You believed in me, and I let you down. I hope the human race comes out on top. With everyone working against each other and not as a team, I don't see that happening. And I'm not meaning the looters. There's so much more to this. Start with who you know. Those who you think are friends are actually your enemies. Don't trust anyone.

Darryl slipped the notebook back into Doug's bag and

followed Ryan, who had stopped at the edge of the creek that spilled into the river. It was completely dry now, the bed thirsty for precipitation.

"You okay?"

Ryan glanced at him from the corner of his eye and didn't respond. Kicking some dirt, dust flew up under his boot and he finally shrugged.

"What the hell does Doug mean by that?" Ryan asked, his brow furrowed with worry.

"I don't know. Could just be evoking more panic. His last attempt at getting back at us for something."

"For me killing his brother?"

This time, Darryl shrugged. "It's hard to say. We didn't know Doug. He stayed private even when he was being talkative. Could've been a huge front. Do we know anyone?"

"I guess we don't. Just another damn reason to get down to what is causing all this catastrophe."

"You don't think it's just the planet finally rebelling against the human race tearing it up?" Darryl was never into that hype, but it seemed like a plausible argument considering their current predicament.

"No." Ryan shook his head and stared out into the pasture. "That can't be the only thing."

"If there's something to be figured out, you're the man to do it," Darryl said, glancing over his shoulder. Steve was still with Doug's body, giving Darryl and Ryan a moment between father and son.

"Am I?" Ryan asked, looking at his father, his eyes red and bloodshot. "Or is this just more bullshit like you said? Doug's last rebellion because I killed his brother. We'll never know. And I don't have the time to go on a wild goose chase to figure out something that might not even exist. It's just more crap to clog up my mind. I wish I could just accept this all for what it is. Mother Nature has gone mad. But I can't let that go, especially after reading a note like that." Ryan pointed back toward Doug and Steve, his jaw set in a hard line.

Darryl looked up at the sky. An orange hue was rising in the east and the beautiful view of the stars was fading.

"The sun will be up soon, Ryan. What should we do with the body?"

Ryan turned on his heel and walked back to Steve, Darryl following behind him. He circled the body, his eyes downcast as they waited for him to answer.

Ryan finally replied, still not making eye contact with either Darryl or Steve. "We'll strip him down, gather his clothes, and whatever he had in the bag. Then we'll bury him. No one needs to see him like this."

CHAPTER SEVEN

T*here's so much more to this.*

Ryan closed his eyes and saw Doug's handwriting, scrawled out on the piece of paper. He had always suspected that more was going on than just global warming and mankind ruining nature but reading someone else's thoughts on it made Ryan's imagination go crazy. When he speculated about it with his father and even Cecilia, he could see the look on their face – they thought he was losing his mind. And maybe he was. Their new way of life was harsh enough to make anyone go insane.

And now, with the suicide of someone they knew, it was more of a reality. Everyone was getting even more desperate as each day passed. Would more people resort to ending their lives?

"What are we going to tell everyone?" Steve asked, glancing at Ryan as the three men walked back toward Harper Springs.

Ryan didn't know so he didn't answer. Ducking his head, he kicked his boot through the dirt, the sand exploding in a large cloud under his weight. It was a good question and unfortunately, one that had to carefully be considered. He didn't want to lie to everyone – it would be easy for someone to figure out the truth about Darryl's death. But Ryan didn't want to put it out there and give others ideas. It was a sensitive time and though suicide was a touchy subject with most people, desperation always made people make hasty decisions that they wouldn't ever consider when things were normal.

"I still want to know why he had his bag with him. Why not leave it behind?" Darryl wondered, shaking his head.

"It's a good thing he had it and we found it. There were some useful things in it," Ryan replied. It came off as uncaring, but it was the world they lived in – it was all about survival, even if it meant pillaging from the corpse of a man you once knew. It was also his way of keeping up a wall. He had his reservations about Doug, but he was developing trust and enjoying the man's sense of humor. Even in that short time, he had gotten attached to him.

"So, we are almost to town. Any ideas?" Steve inquired again, more sensitive about what happened than either Darryl or Ryan.

"We tell everyone he died." Ryan made a quick decision since Darryl and Steve seemed to be waiting for him to make the decision. "It's not a lie."

"They're going to want details, Ryan." Darryl wagged his finger toward Ryan. "You know how it is. When someone that young passes, that's the first thing people ask. What was the cause of death?"

Ryan heaved a deep sigh and looked toward the horizon. The sun was coming up and people were probably already waking up for the day. "Then we tell them the truth if they ask. Only if they ask. There's no sense in giving details voluntarily. But guys, keep the note a secret. That stays completely private."

Steve cocked his head to the side. "Why keep it a secret?"

"Because I need to figure it out, Steve. It could be nothing, but I can't just leave it alone. And with everyone knowing what it says, we may never find out who Doug may be referring to, okay?"

"Got it."

"I have it in my pocket. When I finally get a chance to think and organize my thoughts, I'll see what I can come up with.

Until then, when asked, Doug is dead. If asked how, it was a suicide. That's all that needs to be said."

Steve gave a thumbs up and Darryl shook his head yes in agreement. Ryan patted his pocket, feeling the crumpled paper beneath the top layer of fabric. He trusted Cecilia with his life but he wasn't even going to tell her about it.

Getting back to the cellar was bittersweet. Ryan felt like he could sleep for days but there was too much work to get done. The crops needed watering and he was still researching a way to recycle ammunition. He also wanted to make sure the meat from the wild boars wasn't going bad. Smoking was a great way to preserve it but they also needed to find other ways.

Ryan went straight to the camp shower and washed the dirt off his face. His eyes stung and were dry like sandpaper. Rubbing them, he blinked, and no moisture or tears helped lubricate them.

"Ryan, what happened?"

Turning, he glanced over his shoulder. Cecilia was right behind him, her mouth set in a hard line as she waited for his answer.

"It's Doug, Cecilia," he whispered, turning back to the water. It felt good on his skin and droplets formed on his beard, which was getting long enough for a trim.

"Doug? What happened?"

Turning completely around, Ryan grabbed a towel and dabbed it on his face. Walking to their cots, he lifted the bag of food and pulled out a package of crackers. They were stale but he was starving, so they tasted like a delicacy. Ty was playing with an action figure someone had concocted with wood, oblivious to everyone else.

"Hey, Ty, can you run over there and grab me a package of toothpaste?" Ryan didn't need one but he sent him away for safe measure. Kids heard more than they let on. Turning his attention back to Cecilia, he took her hand and kissed the back of it. "Doug committed suicide."

"He what?" Her eyes widened and she squeezed his hand. "How did..." Biting her bottom lip, she stammered on her words.

"I couldn't sleep. I noticed he was gone and since we were worried he was going to backstab us, I went to see if I could find him. Steve went with me, and we saw him walking." Ryan recounted the details, closing his eyes when he got to the part where Doug completed the deed. "It happened so fast, Cecilia. He did it right in front of us."

"Oh my God..." Cecilia put her hand to her mouth and a single tear trailed down her cheek. "I'm sorry you had to see that. That is so terrible."

"It is." It was on the tip of his tongue to tell her about the note but there were too many people around and he swore to himself he wouldn't bring it up until he could find more out.

"We thought he was going back to the looters. Never would I have imagined it would be suicide."

"We were just going off what we knew about him, Cecilia. Don't feel guilty about that." Ryan stood up and dumped the contents of his bag on the bed. In the past few months, he had gotten into the habit of carrying it everywhere he went. He never knew when he'd have something good to carry home and having it with him helped aid in gathering needed supplies.

"What's all of this?"

"Stuff we got from him. His clothes, boots, and he had a few things in a backpack. The most important is this." Ryan lifted the box of ammunition. "This is more precious than gold now." He dug through everything. He had a hairbrush, thread, needles, and some ibuprofen. It wasn't much but enough not to waste.

"Where is his body?" Cecilia asked.

Ryan watched Ty to make sure he wasn't coming back yet. The child had gotten sidetracked and was playing with one of the other boys he had made friends with.

"We buried him. It's just a shallow grave because the ground is so hard. It won't be long before an animal finds him. They're getting hungry too and coming around. I debated on telling anyone what happened. Thought maybe we could pass it off as him running off. I didn't want everyone to worry about it like I was. Someone would eventually find out and I don't want people to not trust me."

Cecilia cupped the back of his head and kissed his forehead. Her touch was soothing, and it calmed his nerves. "You did the right thing. It's a shame it happened but it's over now."

"I'm going to head up to the crops. They probably need attention." Ryan's mind was racing with the events that had transpired within the past twelve hours. Getting out and working would hopefully help him project that nervous energy into something productive.

Though he was expecting a different outcome, the vegetation was looking strong. Small tomatoes were forming, still a few weeks from being ready to be picked. The corn was growing tall, and the cotton was producing bolls. Ryan walked down the rows like a proud farmer who was about to cash in on his bumper crop. But it was nothing close to a bumper crop – this was the bare minimum that would hopefully get them through the winter months. It was a push in the right direction, and they had to start somewhere. The worry was how harsh the winter was going to be.

Steve joined Ryan on their walk, each surveying the plants and the soil moisture. Ryan was glad he had Steve there. He had gardened before and was brought up around farming, but Steve knew what he was doing. Having his guidance was why they were having success, even if it was minimal.

"It's a good thing the plants are maturing, Ryan. Do you smell that? Fall is here. I would be willing to bet our first freeze is right around the corner."

"That soon, huh?" Ryan knelt and sifted through the leaves on a cotton plant, making sure they weren't being overrun with boll weevils.

"You're the weather guy. But I used to read the farmer's

almanac from cover to cover. If memory serves me right, we are in for an early winter."

Ryan stood up and arched his eyebrow, looking up at the sky. "You remember if it said how harsh the winter was going to be?"

"I think it said the El Nino was going to stick around."

"Shit. Colder and wetter than normal. Wet is fine. Cold, not so much."

Steve was accurate in his speculation – Ryan could smell autumn in the air and the few trees that survived were transitioning with the season. Leaves were turning orange and yellow and starting to fall. The temperature during the day still lingered in the mid-eighties but fell almost thirty degrees when the sun began to set. The days were also getting shorter. Ryan had lost track of what exact day it was. It was about the time of year when time change was about a month away.

That made him think of Thanksgiving and the holidays. A roasted turkey with all the fixings sounded amazing and his stomach growled at the thought of it. Maybe he'd be able to hunt down a wild turkey and they could do their new version of the tradition. With as deprived as they had been of good food, he could probably serve it raw, and everyone would be ready to chow down.

Ryan spent the rest of the day working on the irrigation system. He had gathered some PVC pipe from what remained at the firehouse. He had less to work with than he had anticipated but it still would be enough to use. They would have to move it down the rows throughout the day so someone would have to keep an eye on it.

Using a knife, he carefully carved out small holes on the sides of the pipe. They couldn't be too big or the water would gush out too fast. Too small and the pressure would cause the water to build up and possibly explode the pipe. He also had to be careful not to crack it. One jab into the plastic and it would crack all the way down, ruining it. He didn't have enough to spare to make that mistake.

He had three pipes that were about seven feet long each to use. He didn't have any fittings to piece them together and make an extra-long system, so he could put each pipe down a row in the pasture and move them down as the ground got saturated enough.

Dragging each pipe out, he gently laid them between the rows of corn since it required the most water. He had to position each one downhill to have gravity aid in keeping the water running through each pipe. Luckily, the pasture was on a gradual downhill slope. The water would move slowly but it'd be perfect – it would help the ground absorb the moisture a lot better than just dumping the water on it. The sun would also be less likely to evaporate most of it, allowing them to get more usage out of it. With the dwindling water supply, the creation of the gravity-powered irrigation system came at just the right time.

Ryan grabbed a small bucket and ducked it under the wheelbarrow of water. Lifting the far end of the pipe, he cautiously poured the water in, trying to be as precise as possible, unsure of how it would work or if it even would work. The pipe's circumference was only about four inches total, so he had a small window to work with.

The water swirled downward, and he lay the pipe on the ground. Water flowed out of each intricate hole he made, flowing toward the plants. It wasn't perfect and he needed to come up with a better way to get the water into the pipe, but it'd serve as useful for now.

He continued the process with the other two pipes and stood back, watching his invention come to life. Though it needed some work, Ryan was happy with what he had accomplished. At least the day wasn't a total waste, and he was thrilled that they would be able to start harvesting soon.

As soon as he was finished working, his mind went back to Doug and the note he carried in the pocket of his jeans. Keeping busy was the greatest way he kept his mind off the multiple issues that crept back up.

Start with who you know.

Don't trust anyone.

Ryan pulled the note out and unfolded it, the paper wrinkled from being in his pocket all day. Doug's handwriting flashed up at him. He had the damn thing memorized so there was no need to look at it, but seeing the actual handwriting made it tangible and more realistic.

Start with who you know.

That could be anyone. And start with what? Ryan didn't even know where to begin on it. Though the population of Harper Springs was cut down significantly, it still left several people for him to keep his eye on. He felt like a paranoid psychotic patient who was watching his back against things that didn't even exist.

A gust of wind blew through, almost ripping the suicide note from Ryan's grasp. Clutching it, he slipped it back into his pocket. The air was cold, the temperature instantly dipping at least ten degrees in a matter of seconds. He didn't have a jacket on, so he ran back to the shelter, fighting against the sharp breeze.

Winter was coming. Ryan hoped it'd hold off a few more weeks so they could get their crops to grow a bit bigger before harvest time. A hard freeze would kill everything they had busted their back working on.

Hopefully, *one* thing would go right for them.

CHAPTER EIGHT

Days had passed and Ryan hadn't been able to decipher much out of Doug's note. When he wasn't working on the crops or gathering lumber for the wall, he sat and observed – his surroundings, people, interactions, and behaviors. He felt like a psychology major, studying the human condition. He tried to be inconspicuous, but he probably stuck out like a sore thumb. It was out of the ordinary for him to just sit around. Cecilia had even questioned him because of his unusual behavior.

Nothing seemed strange or out of the ordinary. He didn't want to assume it was a certain person. Even if the note didn't mean a damn thing and Doug was just leading him astray, it was doing its job of rocking Ryan's world. He already had trust issues and now, he was having a hard time trusting most of the people he was working with. He didn't want to become paranoid so much that it crippled his attempt at bettering Harper Springs, which meant he'd have to up his game and start following suspected people.

But what would he be following them for? He didn't even know what he was supposed to be looking for. Were certain people of Harper Springs being two-faced and helping the looters? Would someone be powerful enough to cause the weather to go crazy? No one in Harper Springs would ever be able to pull something like that off. The town was full of good ol' boys and hard-working men – for them to be doing anything shady seemed far-fetched.

He had wasted enough time watching everyone and needed to channel some energy into something productive. Walking to the pile of branches and wood they had stockpiled, he began to sort the good, workable pieces from the ones they could use for something else. They had a good supply of nails gathered from cellars and basements from across the area – it was a stroke of luck that so many people had used their shelters for storage.

The cool breeze picked up and chilled Ryan to the bone. He had been working hard and sweating, and the moisture clung to his back, the air making him shiver against the wet fabric.

"Need a hand?"

Ryan looked up and saw Steve approaching him, tossing him a canteen from a few feet away.

"Yeah, I guess so." Ryan took a swig of water and threw it back at him. "I don't know how we're going to be able to dig holes for the posts. That's going to be the hardest part."

Steve picked up a shovel and tried to break ground but was only successful and moving the top layer of sand around. "Jeez, it's like there's a layer of concrete right under us."

"And we really can't spare much more water to soften the ground. It'd take a lot."

"We could use your irrigation system to do it if you wanted."

Ryan nodded and tried his attempt at digging a hole. Putting his weight on the back of it, the shovel was able to sink in an inch before the dirt rejected it.

"I don't know."

"I guess we have to decide if building a wall will be that important to our safety. Will it keep people out?"

Ryan glanced down at the pile of wood. Most of it was broken tree branches and pieces of debris found in fields that had been flung off of barns and houses.

"We might not even have enough to go around the whole town. And look at it." Ryan motioned toward it with his hand. "It's already weakened from the damage it sustained from the tornadoes. If someone wanted to get through, they'd have no problem. I don't think using more of our water supply would be a good idea."

"Well, there you go. I think you made up your mind on that." Steve looked toward the pasture, his eyes widening. "What about putting a fence around our crops?"

"Yeah?"

"Yeah. It'll help keep the wildlife out. And the ground is already softened from watering. It won't protect us but at least we won't lose as many plants to animals."

"Good idea. Rabbits can probably still get through, but it'll deter deer and other things from romping through it." They had lost a few plants to animals coming toward town, looking for something to eat. With the plants finally producing vegetables, they'd be coming around a lot more.

Ryan and Steve began lugging the wood closer to the pasture. The shovel went in the ground much easier, still hitting harder ground just half a foot down but it was better to work with. And best of all, it wouldn't dip into the water supply.

They began by putting in stronger branches that word serve as the posts to hold up the fence. Some wood splintered and fractured as soon as they drove a nail through. Sitting in standing water eroded a lot of it but they'd have just enough to span around the perimeter of their garden.

"What in the hell are y'all doing?" Chief Rayburn's voice boomed as he approached them on horseback.

Ryan continued to work, digging holes just deep enough for the posts to be stable. "Building a fence, Mike." Using his Chief's first name still felt funny. He was no longer Ryan's superior. Their previous encounter left a bitter taste in Ryan's mouth and with their world turned upside down, everyone was on a level playing field. No one outranked anyone else.

"I thought we were using all of this to go around the town?" Mike asked, sliding off the side of his horse.

"The ground is too hard, and we don't have enough. This will help keep most of the wildlife out of here."

"And how do you propose we protect the town? You know those looters aren't done, don't you?"

"Of course, I know that Mike. Do you think a fence is going to steer them away?"

"You seem to be developing a load of confidence in all of this, aren't you?" Mike stepped forward and Ryan refused to back down. He stood several inches taller than Ryan, and Ryan wasn't a small man. But Ryan wasn't going to be bullied. "I think you're enjoying what is happening to everyone, aren't you?"

Steve stood by Ryan's side, neither of them moving. It was a random confrontation and Ryan couldn't believe how much a man he used to serve on the fire department with had changed. Considering the circumstances, all of them had changed but most for the better. It was a shame the toll it was taking on them.

"You're kidding me, right?" Ryan shook his head and turned to continue to work. He didn't have time to stand around and fight.

Mike grabbed his shirt, pulling him to face him again, getting close enough to Ryan that their noses were almost touching. Gritting his teeth, Mike, gripped his shirt so tight that the fibers of cotton would rip at any moment.

"I'm not kidding, no. You think you're running this show, don't you? Who died and made you stud dick?"

"No one. I'm trying to get us all to work together."

"You're trying to run the show."

Ryan pulled away from Mike and the grip he had on his shirt was lost. It was stretched out and Ryan had to adjust it on his shoulder. "There is no show to run, Mike. This is survival and we all have to do our part. Common sense says we don't have enough supplies to build a fence around Harper Springs. The ground is too hard, and it would be a waste. Now's not the time for a damn power struggle."

Mike laughed but it wasn't out of amusement. His expression was haunting like the man was completely losing his mind. Ryan hoped that wasn't true – the image of Doug blowing his brains out was enough. He didn't want someone else going through the same mental turmoil.

"This is all a waste, Gibson. Go ahead and have your fun. Make yourself feel big by making decisions for everyone."

"What the hell is that supposed to mean?" Ryan stepped forward but Steve put his hand on Ryan's chest, stopping him. He was thankful for that – he needed a voice of reason amid his anger.

"Read between the lines, Gibson." Mike climbed back on his horse and trotted it, glancing over his shoulder before getting out of earshot. "Read between the fucking lines."

Ryan watched him ride off until he couldn't see him again, going south, away from Harper Springs. First Doug's note – now Mike's strange comments. It was all a mind game and if anyone was losing their sanity, Ryan felt like he was. *Read between the lines.* As if he wasn't confused before, he was now.

❄

"AT LEAST THERE is one thing positive about all of this," Mindy said as she snuggled up next to Steve.

"What's that?"

"The evenings are cool now and the stars are beautiful. Fall has always been my favorite season."

"I'm more of a spring guy."

"Why? What makes you like spring?"

Steve laid back on the blanket and looked up at the sky. The sun was going down behind the mountains, the breeze was almost too cool, and the small talk with Mindy was great to get his mind off the scene that played out just a few hours ago between Ryan and Chief Rayburn. He tried not to let it distract him – seeing a collapse in the friendship between the two men was worrisome. If everyone started fighting, their future in Harper Springs could become compromised.

"Planting season starts. Warmer weather. And believe it or not, I did love storm season."

"Did being the operative word, right?"

"I guess so. I guess what has happened to us would make anyone gun shy about it." He pulled her in close and kissed the top of her head. Beginning a romance with someone during everything wasn't exactly great timing but as everyone kept saying, life must go on. This was his way of moving forward, and Mindy was fun to be around. She was the first woman to make him have butterflies in his stomach since his ex-wife, and the last few years of that marriage were nothing short of hell.

"I like fall because of the foliage. Trees are turning beautiful colors. Things are going into hibernation. It's nature's way of sort of taking a break," Mindy said as she traced her index finger over Steve's chest.

"Fall means more work for me. Harvest time, stripping season, and I hate winter. It's just the winter's eve and I've never liked the cold."

Mindy rolled onto her side and leaned on her elbow. "What kind of winter do you think we're in for?"

"Ryan seems to think it'll be a cold one. The Farmer's Almanac is consistent with his prediction."

"But it's just a prediction, yeah?" Mindy looked away, biting her bottom lip. Her brow creased and she looked like she was on the verge of crying.

"Yeah, of course. He's been right through all of this, though. He knew the drought was going to happen just days after the tornadoes stopped. So, anything he says about the weather, I pretty much take to the bank. He knows what he's talking about."

"Was he a weather guy before all of this happened?" Mindy

inquired, sliding to her back again, her warm body pressed up against his.

"No. I think he was a mechanic."

"Ah. Well, then there's hope he could be wrong about winter."

"Yeah, I guess so. It's a catch twenty-two. We need snow to help replenish the lakes. Better yet, if it'd stay above freezing, the rain would be fine too. I just don't know what the hell to expect."

They lay in silence for a few minutes. The crickets chirped, the wind rustled around them, and the temperature dipped quickly. Steve snuggled against Mindy, unwilling to move. He wasn't ready to go back to the shelter. The fresh air was doing them well and his time alone with her was a break from the real world.

"So, what gives, Steve? What is bothering you tonight?"

"What makes you think something is bothering me?"

"You're usually optimistic, having something positive to say about everything we talk about. It's a nice balance to counteract my negativity. I can just tell. Everything go okay today?"

This time, Steve moved onto his side, facing her. He studied her face, wishing he could have met her under other circumstances. "Just thinking about the past few days. Doug's suicide. Ryan's argument with Mike Rayburn. The changing of the seasons around us. Sorry if I'm not seeming like myself."

Mindy's eyes widened again, and she sat up, dusting the dirt from her clothes. "Ryan had a fight with Mike Rayburn? Over what?"

Steve shrugged. "It was stupid. Rayburn accused him of wanting to take over. Bullshit like that happens when there isn't a government. One man wants to undermine the other. For some reason, Mike thinks he's appointed to the top of the totem pole and we're just going to fall in and obey it. But he hasn't done much. He doesn't make crucial decisions and he's always missing in action. I haven't seen him do much to help lately. And people notice that. Why would we want a leader like that?"

"You're an American, Steve. Isn't that what it takes to be a politician? Sit on your ass while the rest of the country busts theirs?" Mindy giggled and nudged him. "Are you saying we need to have an election? Do we need to appoint a leader?"

"I never thought it'd get to that but maybe, yeah..." Steve replied. "I don't know what Ryan's opinion would be, but he'd have my vote if it came down to it."

"What makes you think he'd want to do it?"

"He's already sort of stepped into the role, unofficially, even if Mike Rayburn doesn't agree. A vote would make it official. Maybe with some sense of law and order, everyone would feel a little safer."

Mindy intertwined her fingers in his and smiled. "You ought to bring it up. You never know. And between you and me... I'd vote for you."

"Nah. I'm not qualified. Ryan is from the area. Everyone knows him. He'd do a much better job."

"Then you can be his assistant. Or I guess if you stick to the great American tradition, his vice president. You two make a good team."

"I'd be more suited for the head of agriculture," Steve replied, this time, he laughed, and it felt good.

Mindy nudged him again and leaned in, kissing him. Falling back against the hard ground, Steve enjoyed their warm embrace, her weight on top of him, and the emotions that coursed through him. It made him feel alive and normal. And for a few minutes, the worry of the past few days had dissipated, even if it was just temporary.

CHAPTER NINE

Due to his continued insomnia, Ryan rose early to work. A few more days had passed and with the temperatures plummeting faster than normal, he began harvesting the vegetables, some still not mature enough, but the weather was threatening, and he'd rather have smaller ears of corn and tomatoes than a hard freeze coming through, completely ruining everything.

He didn't pick it all, leaving some bit of hope that winter would hold off and they'd get full-sized plants to use. Sifting through the vegetation, he plucked vegetables from every other plant, giving them some food supply, leaving the rest behind to grow a little more, edging out as much as they could before it was too late.

The moon was still bright overhead, and the wind was cool on his skin. The tornadoes had wiped out everything, including any winter clothing they had stored up in their homes. They were lucky to have blankets – no one had coats and that was posing a new problem. The shelter was warm thanks to everyone's body heat but as it got colder, the ground temperature would get cold along with it. They could heat their living area with propane stoves and heaters, but they had to ration that as well.

After finishing with the corn, Ryan moved down the row to the tomato plants. They were only producing at about the size of cherries. He'd take what he could get. His heart skipped a beat when he heard the clomp of horse hooves a few yards away. His initial thought was that the looters were back, and he ducked inside the tall corn to hide.

Peering through the stalks, he tried to spot whoever it might be. He always carried his handgun with him wherever he went and had it readily available in case the situation turned dangerous. He couldn't tell who the person was on the horse at first. Whoever it was had a heavy coat on and a scarf that covered their face. How in the hell had they come across winter wear like that? Judging by the size of the person, it was a man.

Crawling on his hands and knees, Ryan moved down the row of corn, trying hard not to move the stalks as he pushed through them. The man on the horse wasn't going fast, which helped Ryan keep a good watch on him. If only he'd uncover his face, Ryan could see who it was. If he was with the looter group, he was alone, which meant he was probably a spy – which also meant they were planning a move-in on Harper Springs soon.

Squinting his eyes, the orange hue of dawn was aiding in keeping the identity of the person hidden. The man stopped the horse completely and Ryan held his breath in fear that the stranger had heard him. But there was no way that was possible. He was far enough away unless Ryan was shaking the corn stalks more than he had thought. Maybe the man would assume it was an animal picking away at the plants and there was nothing to worry about.

He finally pulled his scarf down and looked over his shoulder. The hair on the back of Ryan's neck stood up when he got a clear look at the man's face. It was Mike Rayburn. The only question now was, where was he headed so early in the morning and how had he gotten his hands on the winter supplies he had on him?

Ryan considered following him. The man was on horseback so it might prove to be challenging. He could hurry and grab one, but it'd be a dead giveaway and he wouldn't be able to hide. Crouching in the corn, he continued to watch Mike. He wasn't riding fast and stopped now and then. It'd be a huge risk, and no one would know where he was if he followed.

Running his hand down his pocket, Ryan felt the outline of his gun. It was his security blanket and though it was probably a mistake, made him feel invincible. It was haunting, thinking about how much he had changed – used to, he'd never immediately resort to grabbing a weapon but now it was second nature when he was in harm's way. His fight or flight response was going full force and he was glad to know that he chose fight over flight.

Ryan stayed low to the ground and inched out of the corn. Mike was about a thousand yards up ahead and if he didn't pick up his pace, he would lose sight of him. Maybe that was a good thing. This wasn't exactly a well thought out plan. What would he say to Mike if he caught him? There was no out story or easy way to explain that he was following him because he didn't trust him any further than he could throw him.

From the looks of it, Mike was headed toward his ranch. Ryan would assume that since he couldn't keep up on foot. As soon as he hit the open farmland, he ran the horse fast, disappearing over the top of a foothill. Ryan considered continuing – Mike's ranch was only about two miles away from where the outskirts of Harper Springs used to be. He could make that walk fast – due to all the physically demanding work, a two-mile trek was easy.

Looking up at the moon, he estimated that there were still a few hours before the sun would come up. That would give him ample time to check it out and make it back without alarming Cecilia. She had become overly protective of him, and he couldn't blame her.

Since Mike was out of sight, Ryan didn't worry about staying low to the ground. And now he had a back story if his former chief decided to circle back around and catch him out there. He could just claim he was gathering supplies and happened onto Mike's former ranch. The way Ryan saw it, no one owned any land anymore. Just like no one held a higher rank over the other. They were all equal, fighting for the same thing – life and survival.

He made a personal note to watch for rattlesnakes. It was starting to get a little cool for them, but he couldn't risk it. The dry tumbleweeds were prime places they liked to hide, and the open land was packed full of them. If a good gust of wind came through it would look like an old, dusty western.

He also had to keep an eye out for wildlife. Just like people were becoming desperate, so were animals, and they were getting brave enough to get closer and closer to places they once never considered prowling at. Mountain lions had been spotted coming down toward town and there were also added threats of wild boars, foxes, and coyotes.

Ryan tried to keep his pace up. He was able to walk a mile in a little under ten minutes now so it would take about twenty to get to the old Rayburn place. Since he had to watch every step he took, he reached Mike's property line fast, his palms becoming sweaty when he saw the horse Mike had been riding tied up to a set of mangled trees beside the foundation where his ranch house once stood. But where was Mike?

Ryan looked for a place to hide but all the shrubbery and trees had been picked thin and he was left vulnerable, standing out in the middle of the yard with the bright moon cascading right down on top of him. It was likely that Mike had gone down into his basement and Ryan ran to another grove of trees just south of the house. He felt dirty for spying on his former chief but something about him was making his skin crawl.

Crouching again, he was glad his clothes were dark. If he stayed still, maybe Mike would never know he was being watched. He held his breath when he spotted Mike walking up the steps, a large object in his arms. Balancing on the last step, he gained his footing and set it down. Ryan couldn't tell what it was, but Mike quickly went back down the stairs.

He wanted to give Rayburn the benefit of the doubt. Maybe he was gathering more supplies to help Harper Springs. Maybe he had found some stuff he had forgotten about. But Ryan's instincts were saying otherwise – he just wanted to know what in the hell this man was up to.

He waited a few more seconds – Mike came back up again empty-handed and took a long swig from a bottle. It wasn't a canteen, and it didn't take a genius to figure out he had tapped into some alcohol. Ryan longed for a drink. It had been months since he had tasted the heavy flavor of whiskey burning down to his stomach. Not to mention how great it would be to aid in easing his anxiety. Watching Mike wasn't helping and now he was stuck. He willed Mike to go back down into the basement so he could run off. Now wasn't the time or place to confront him. He needed solid ground to say something and right now, for all Ryan knew, Mike was just gathering supplies. He couldn't just point fingers and claim the man was up to no good.

Mike finished off the bottle and tossed it aside, the glass clanking against the box he had lugged up the stairs. Inching back downward, Ryan waited a few seconds and took the chance to run back toward town.

Following Mike hadn't helped a bit. Instead, it opened more curiosity that Ryan feared he'd never get answers to. All he was doing was moving a big box. Ryan wasn't in a position to assume anything, but Mike's recent behavior was enough of a red flag to make him question everything the man did.

Read between the lines.

Mike's words echoed in Ryan's mind. Reading between the lines was going to make him lose his mind. Everyone was a suspect. He just had to figure out exactly what it was that they might be guilty of.

❄

Cecilia woke up and reached out for Ryan, but his cot was empty. Sitting up, she wiped the sleep from her eyes and squinted. It was completely dark and only a few lanterns were burning. She had no idea what time it was, but it was too early for him to be out and about. Most people had become early risers and if no one was stirring, it was likely still in the morning hours.

Sighing, she hoped he was just using the bathroom or got hungry. Waiting a few minutes, she listened to Ty's breathing on the cot adjacent to them. Sometimes he'd snore and his nostrils would whistle, and it made her smile. He was getting more active, which meant he always crashed hard when it was time to go to bed. There was rarely any argument out of him when they called lights out.

Kicking her legs over the side, her toes touched the cool floor beneath her. Where in the hell was Ryan? She couldn't take much more of him going out there in the middle of danger, and now he wasn't communicating with her. She knew Ryan could hold his own, but she was a worrier – if something happened to him she'd be devastated. Ty wouldn't understand. And most importantly, he had stepped into a leadership role without even trying. How would the people of Harper Springs respond if he got killed or completely disappeared? It'd be a complete collapse of society – and she thought they had already hit rock bottom with current conditions.

Ambling toward the toiletry table, Cecilia felt her way around everyone. Some people had to sleep on the floor, some in chairs, and a few people were awake, whispering or lying there staring off into the darkness.

Nodding toward a few of them, she felt comfortable now that her eyes had started adjusting to the darkness. Muscle memory was helpful – if there came a day when they moved things around, she was certain she'd be bumping into more than she was at that moment.

"Cecilia?"

She heard Darryl's whisper a few steps away and it made her jump.

"Darryl?"

"What are you doing up?"

"I can ask you the same question," she replied, smoothing her hands over her hair.

"I couldn't sleep."

Cecilia ducked her head and ran her hand over the surface of the snack table. "Ryan isn't on his cot."

"What?"

"He's not there. Do you know where he went?"

Darryl shrugged, his eyes widening. "No. Maybe he's just working."

"In the dark?"

"Yeah. The full moon makes it bright enough to get some of the harvest done. And if I know Ryan, if he can't sleep, he's going to make himself useful."

Cecilia wrapped her baggy shirt around her, hugging her midsection. The transition to cooler air was abrupt and they weren't quite equipped for the change of seasons. The thin blankets the clinic had supplied would help but probably wouldn't be enough if winter came down on them hard.

"I wish he'd tell me these things."

Darryl patted her arm. "I know. He probably just didn't want to wake you."

She wouldn't be able to go back to sleep, so she gathered a few items for breakfast. Ty was still hooked on instant oatmeal, and she couldn't stomach the thought of eating another bite of it. They had pulled out some of the boar meat and she considered warming some of it up. Under normal circumstances she would have never considered eating it – fear of food contamination would have made her completely avoid it – but now, her mouth watered at the thought of the smoky meat.

They stored it in the wall of a cellar, keeping it cool, and it had been smoked – the chances that it would have any issues were slim. It didn't have all the added chemicals and preservatives that store-bought meat had, which was good and bad. It was all organic, which meant it was probably safer than anything she had cooked before all of this had happened.

Cecilia lit the lantern near her cot, the heat of the match burning her fingertips. Blowing it out quickly, she winced at the shot of pain. She put her finger in her mouth and made sure her whimper hadn't woken anyone up. Ty and her mother slept soundly, and she didn't see where Darryl had wandered off to.

Pulling the camp stove out, she made sure to be more careful when lighting the burner. The propane bottle they were using was low, so she'd have to be quick in warming food up. They had stored some of the meat in the shelter in tightly sealed bags submerged in water to keep it cool.

Dumping the meat into the small frying pan, she moved it around with a spoon, the scent of it wafting upward, making her stomach growl. They were all malnourished and losing a lot of weight. Even if she wanted to gobble down a lot of food, her stomach wouldn't allow it. It had shrunk and she was good for a few bites here and there.

Margaret sat up on her cot and squinted toward Cecilia, rubbing her eyes with her fist. "Cecilia?"

"Good morning."

"What are you doing?" She whispered, her eyes averting to Ty and back to her daughter.

"Cooking some breakfast. Are you hungry?"

"I am. What time is it?"

"I'm not sure. It's still early yet but I couldn't sleep."

She knew that the scent of her cooking would start to wake others up. If she had to estimate it, it was almost time for everyone to start getting up anyway.

"Something is on your mind, isn't it?" Margaret approached her, cupping Cecilia's chin in her palm.

"Of course, Mom. It doesn't take a genius to figure that out."

She cringed at how harsh it sounded. “I’m sorry, Mom. I don’t mean to sound so hateful.”

“It’s quite alright, honey. Talk to me. I’m here for you.”

Cecilia flipped over the pieces of meat, hoping that if she got it warmed up well enough, it’d completely wipe out the chances of making them sick. There was still a part of her that didn’t trust it.

“It’s all fine, Mom. I can’t dump things all on you when you are...” She cut herself off and looked away, feeling the warmth in the corners of her eyes. She didn’t want to cry in front of anyone.

“When I am what?” Margaret asked, taking the plastic spoon from Cecilia.

“When you’re going through your own stuff. Dad...” No matter how hard she tried to control it, the tears flowed, and she tried to swipe them away as soon as they trailed down her cheeks.

“It’s all going to be okay, Cecilia.”

“Hell, look at me, Mom. I didn’t think I had any tears left in me to cry.”

Margaret took Cecilia’s arm and pulled her in, wrapping her arms around her in a tight hug. Cecilia buried her face against her mom, the embrace warm, comforting, and a jolt into reality. She didn’t know what she’d do without her mother, and she had come close to losing her. It was hard enough knowing what happened to her father. Losing her mom would completely kill her.

“This is life as we know it now, Mom. I just can’t accept it.”

Margaret held both sides of Cecilia’s face in her hands and kissed her forehead, her kind and gentle smile just like Cecilia remembered when she was a child. “I know, honey. It’s a bad dream we can’t seem to wake up from.”

Cecilia held onto her mother for a while, unwilling to let her go. For that split second, she didn’t have to face reality. She was a little girl again, safe in her mother’s arms, putting life on hold for as long as she could.

CHAPTER TEN

Ryan estimated he'd be back in Harper Springs in time for everyone to start waking up. He wanted to be there when Cecilia and Ty got up and possibly make them breakfast. If his wife got wind of him jaunting off on a random trip following Mike Rayburn, she'd be very upset with him, especially since he didn't tell anyone where he was going. Not to mention the fact that he suspected his former Chief of something – he just wasn't quite sure what it was yet.

The trek back would be fast if he kept moving. Checking over his shoulder every few feet, he wanted to make sure Rayburn wasn't on his trail or had spotted him. So far so good but the next time he looked to the west, the sight behind him stopped him in his tracks.

Ducking low against a large boulder, Ryan's heart skipped a beat. He couldn't believe what he was seeing. This couldn't be happening, especially not so soon. A large squall line was fast approaching, coming over the top of the mountains. The sun normally was starting to come up by now, but the dark clouds swirled, keeping the area under nightfall. It was kicking up dust beneath it – the thirsty ground was easily lifted by the wind. A wall of dirt formed much like the one they had gotten caught in on their way to Fox Lake to find Cecilia's parents.

Staying low, Ryan tried to watch as long as he could. He thought about running but it was coming so fast that there would be no outrunning it, even if he tried. He searched for a ravine or a low spot to hide but there wasn't anything. The boulder would be the best thing to hopefully protect him from whatever the squall line had in store for him.

He watched on as long as he could. Dirt flew in, stinging his skin, painful against his face like a burn from a fire. He was scared to close his eyes – he wanted to make sure nothing would fly toward him, but it was impossible. Along with the flying dust, the temperature fell drastically in a matter of seconds, the cold bearing down on him like a bucket of ice.

It wasn't a typical fall temperature – there was no doubt that it dipped well below freezing. Ryan's teeth chattered, his body completely unprotected from the sudden fluctuation in weather. His jeans and light jacket were no match for it. With the high winds, the wind chill made it feel like it was below zero. If he didn't do something soon, he'd suffer from possible frostbite or hypothermia.

The dust was beginning to settle but the wind didn't let up. Ryan slowly opened his eyes, getting his first look around him. The dark clouds continued to swirl overhead, growling like they were a monster ready to devour whatever stood in their way.

Rolling on his back, Ryan watched the anomaly overhead. He was awestruck by the beauty wrapped in the danger of the situation. It wasn't tornadic so he didn't have to worry about that, but it was dangerous. He was lucky the wind hadn't done more.

And then the sleet began to fall, the tiny white balls of icy precipitation pelting him in the face. At first, he welcomed it. It was moisture that would help replenish vegetation and the river. He laid back and admired the show that Mother Nature was providing for him, lying flat on his back on the dusty ground. It was hypnotic, sending Ryan deep into a trance. The gray, black, and white swirls of the storm made it appear like a painting, touched by the hand of Michelangelo himself.

Snapping out of it, he sat up, realizing the reality of the situation. Sleet meant below-freezing temperatures. Below-freezing temperatures meant that vegetation would die. And they weren't close to finishing the harvest yet.

Forcing himself to a standing position, Ryan ran, fighting against the wind and sleet that stung just as bad as the dust had a few minutes ago. The cold air was hard on his lungs, and he felt the burn deep inside, his dry cough unproductive. Ignoring all his body's warnings to stop, he sprinted, weaving in and out of tree stumps and hills.

The sleet and wind continued, following him step by step. His muscles ached from the cold, his legs weak as he urged them to continue to move. He had no way of telling which way the storm was going or if it was even moving toward Harper Springs. The fact that it came out of the west was even more strange – usually, cold fronts flew in from the north, coming down from Canada, gaining momentum over middle America, and hitting their part of Texas before completely dying out.

Harper Springs was just over the next hill. Ryan clenched his teeth and ran as fast as he could. The storm hadn't let up, which meant that their small pasture was getting hit with the winter weather. If he got there fast and got help from some of the other men, he'd be able to salvage the vegetables and plants that already had been produced. If this didn't turn into a hard freeze, it might not do too much damage if they could find a way to get the plants covered up. If they could squeeze out a few more weeks off them, that would help their surplus of food.

Running down the hill, he approached the pasture, skipping past it and onto the shelter. Pulling the door open, others were awake, but no one seemed to realize what was happening overhead. The sleet was about a half-inch deep on the ground with no signs of stopping anytime soon.

"Steve!" Ryan spotted him and yelled down. "Steve, I need your help! Now!"

Everyone looked up at him, but no one asked questions. Not only did Steve come up the stairs, but several other men joined them at ground level. Ryan felt confident in knowing he had the help needed to get the work done. What was even more shocking was that no one had commented on the sudden turn in the weather. Instead, they all went to work, knowing exactly what they needed to accomplish.

Saving the plants and harvesting the vegetables was the top priority. All of Ryan's other worries were placed on the back burner temporarily.

Fighting the bitter cold that chilled him to the bone, Ryan pulled vegetables and fruit from plants, even if it wasn't quite ready. It was better than nothing and the weather would kill it if they left it on the plant. Steve and another man carried light sheets to cover some of the more fragile plants, but the wind was blowing hard enough that it would easily be blown off if they didn't weigh it down.

Ryan grabbed some gravel from a nearby pile, thanking himself for stacking it nearby. It was the rock he had found in the ground while tilling for the garden and at that time, he had no idea what he'd use it for, but now it'd serve a good purpose as a weight to keep the covers on the plants.

"I don't know if this will help but at least it'll protect the plants from windburn," Steve said, yelling over the roar of the wind.

"Might as well give it a try," Ryan replied, taking a step back to catch his breath. "Where did the covers come from? Is someone going to be without blankets tonight? Looks like it's going to be cold. I think this is the official unofficial start to winter if you catch my drift."

"Off of my cot and a couple of other guy's cots. It'll be fine. We've got a couple of propane heaters we can kick on. At least the wind chill won't be so bad down in the cellar."

Ryan nodded and weaved in and out of the rows, double-checking what wasn't covered to make sure they hadn't left things that were ready to pick behind. There was a large bucket full of cotton bolls they could hopefully work off. He wasn't sure if there was anyone in the group that would know how to sew or work with it but there was always a time to learn. They had saved the skin from the boars he had killed – if anything, they could try to concoct something out of those things. It wouldn't be big enough for a large blanket, but they could make hats, gloves, or other winter-type protection.

Hoisting the buckets, Ryan carried four down, dangling the handles over his arms as he went. Steve rolled a wheelbarrow toward the cellar they had deemed their storage for garden pickings and animals they had hunted. Stacking everything in the far corner, Ryan inventoried everything in front of him, trying not to feel discouraged at the forced harvest.

It was quite a bit of food. The burning question was if it would last them through the winter. There was no way to know the answer to that. Even if they had a massive surplus there was no way to know. The weather was far too unpredictable to be able to gauge when the cold snap would end. The normal span of winter in their area was usually December until almost the end of February, sometimes into mid-March. Even before Mother Nature had gone completely crazy, they never knew what to expect when it came to the length of winter or how drastic it would be.

"Do you think it'll get warm again before it is all said and done?" Steve asked, both men staring at the unorganized pile of wood.

"I wish I knew," Ryan replied. "Guess it's best to prepare for the worst. Which means this isn't going to get us halfway through. We're going to run out."

"Maybe the plants will survive and give us a little more."

Ryan glanced at Steve and back to their stockpile, a sense of dread settling in the pit of his stomach as if he had just swallowed a brick. All their hard work in rushing to get the crops planted was quickly smashed by the evilness happening overhead. He could still hear the sleet falling, bouncing against the metal door of the cellar.

"We're gonna have to hunt more often. If it snows, we can store it in the ice. If not, we can take our chances like we've been doing with the pork we have. We should probably get to the salt lake soon. There were plans to harvest salt out of it but I don't think anyone ever went that way," Ryan said, spouting off orders to whoever would listen.

He still wondered how in the hell he had gotten into a position where they were listening to him. He was just as green as they were when it came to prepping and surviving. This was like a survival reality show, only there were no cameras and people behind the scenes to bail them out when the going got tough.

Hunting meant using ammunition, which brought up the question of making their own. Ryan knew how to do it – he did it often back when he had supplies in his garage. That was also when he had gunpowder, shells, and plenty to work with.

"How much ammunition do we have, Steve? Ballpark figure."

"Depends on which gun you're wanting to use."

"Shotguns, rifles, things we can hunt with."

"I think we are in good shape with those. The only shots we've had to take were when you killed those pigs and when..." Steve stopped himself and looked away, dodging eye contact with Ryan.

"When I killed Doug's brother and the man with rabies." Ryan finished his sentence, lowering his voice. He hadn't thought about those deaths in a while and the subject made the imaginary brick he had swallowed just minutes before even heavier in his stomach.

"It sure is helpful that a lot of people around here used their basements and cellars as their gun cabinets. If it wasn't for that, we'd only have the bullets the guns were loaded with before the tornadoes hit."

Ryan shook his head and agreed, forcing a smile. "Almost seems too convenient." With the lingering threat of the looters still circling Harper Springs, they had to save what they could in the means of weapons and protection. He'd have to go as far as rationing even that, which meant whoever went hunting would have to have bull's eye aim. They couldn't afford to waste a single bullet, just like they couldn't afford to let a single piece of fruit or vegetable go to waste.

Taking the stairs back up to ground level, Ryan's first observation was that the sleet had transitioned to heavy snow. The wind had died down, but the air was still very cold, making him shiver due to lack of warm clothing. He took a second to admire it – it was a blessing and a curse all in one.

Heading back to the main shelter, Ryan joined his family that was awake and eating. Cecilia greeted him with a smile and hugged him and Ty followed suit, clutching his leg.

"Daddy, is it really snowing?"

"It is. Lots of it." Ryan tried to act like everything was okay, but Cecilia stood back, the look on her face proving that she was onto him. Her brow creased and her smile quickly faded.

Ryan followed her away from Ty, his father, and Margaret and Cecilia wiped a couple of snowflakes from his shoulder. Neither spoke at first – Ryan wasn't sure what to say and Cecilia was likely waiting for him to break the silence.

"Do you know how to can vegetables without a pressure cooker?" he asked, getting to the point. She was mad about something, and he didn't have time for marriage drama.

"I need a pot with water in it and a way to boil it. It's not as safe as if I had a pressure cooker, though."

"Not as safe? What do you mean?"

"Boiling it won't get it hot enough to possibly kill botulism. A pressure cooker gets hot enough. But doing a boiling water bath will seal the jars and keep it fresher than just letting it sit to rot."

"So, there is a chance that we could get botulism if we can everything?" Ryan asked, the discouragement growing.

"Yeah, a little, but what other choice do we have? Has anyone found a pressure cooker? How many vegetables and fruit are we talking about?"

"Not as much as I hoped we would get, but enough that will go bad if we don't do something about it."

Cecilia folded her arms over her chest and took a deep breath, glancing past Ryan at other people as they talked about the weather change.

"We can take our chances with the boiling water bath. It'd be a shame if it all went bad if we didn't do something. When we cook the vegetables, we'll just have to make sure we do it thoroughly. That'll help tremendously. We can also put a little salt in them to help with acidity. That's important when it comes to killing off any food-borne illnesses."

"Good," Ryan replied, putting his hands on her shoulders, kissing her forehead. "We have those jars we found at your parent's cellar – that should be enough, but if not, there is another box somewhere around here. We can get started on that as soon as the snow tapers off some... if the snow tapers off some," Ryan said, correcting himself. He was good at predicting tornadoes and droughts. Winter weather was a whole new ball game he wasn't the best at.

"Happy to help, Ryan." Cecilia smiled. "And when we have a moment, we're going to talk about what's on your mind. Something is bugging you. I can tell."

Ryan didn't respond to her observation. He had never been able to hide anything from her, and his concern about what Mike Rayburn was up to was no exception. He had to be careful what he disclosed to people, including his wife. He trusted her completely but until he got it all figured out, he'd have to keep it concealed. There was too much risk involved off of what ifs and speculation.

CHAPTER ELEVEN

Cecilia kept a close eye on Ryan for most of the morning. She felt like a stalker, watching him without his knowledge and attempting to not be so obvious to others. It was a challenge with them all cramped up around each other in the shelter. The snow continued to fall and with no real winter clothing, Ryan's hands were tied when it came to going out and getting some work done.

The storm shelter was a little cold but the body temperature of everyone inside helped keep it from getting too miserable. The biggest issue was everyone getting cabin fever. It was times like this that Cecilia loved putting something in the slow cooker or whipping up a beef roast. The thought of snuggling on the couch with a good book or movie made her mood crash downward. Instead, she looked around – kids were getting cranky, parents were annoyed, and Ryan couldn't sit still.

She watched him pace back and forth, following the perimeter of the small box they were all trapped in. Someone would talk to him, and he'd nod, pass by, and keep walking. It wasn't just the weather and not getting any work done that was making Ryan act that way. She had known him for years – something was bugging him. One thing she had learned was the way to approach it with him. Sometimes his defenses were up and sometimes he'd vent away. There was no real process to tell what kind of mood he would be in.

Taking him a cup of coffee, Cecilia handed it to him and tried to corner him. To her surprise, he stopped without much effort on her part and took a long sip from the cup. She waited a few seconds, aware of his delicate mood and his frustration. It had been so long since she had seen a genuine smile on his face.

"Everything okay, Ryan?"

He nodded and finished the coffee, wiping his mouth with the back of his hand. "We're wasting time just sitting around here."

"What do you suggest we do? If you go out there, you're going to get frostbite."

"So, we just sit on our asses through the whole winter? We can't let things get behind. We've got vegetables to can and..."

Cecilia put her index finger over his lips to quiet him down. Leaning in, she replaced her lips where her finger was and gently kissed him, hoping the seductive route might help her edge when it came to getting him to talk.

"You've been working non-stop for days, Ryan. When are you gonna tell me what else is going on in that head of yours?"

Ryan's eyes darted around the room and stopped when his gaze met hers. Leaning back against the wall, he heaved a deep sigh and closed his eyes. Cecilia was right in her assumption – it went well beyond his worry about staying busy. It was something bigger than she could imagine and she pondered if she even wanted to know. Sometimes ignorance was bliss, but this involved her husband. She had to know – if anything, to keep him out of harm's way as best as she could.

"I..." Ryan trailed off, looking around the room again. "I can't talk about it here."

"Why?"

"Too many people around."

Cecilia took his hand and kissed the back of it. "That bad, huh?"

"I'm not sure yet."

Cecilia arched her eyebrow and laughed, though she didn't mean to. "Listen to yourself, Ryan. If you're not sure, then why are you letting whatever it is drive you so crazy?"

"I can't explain it." He tightened his grip on her hand. "Have you seen Mike?"

"Mike who?"

"Mike Rayburn." His tone was filled with annoyance and Cecilia legitimately didn't know who Mike was until Ryan said his last name.

"What happened to calling him Chief?"

Ryan's brow furrowed and his mouth set in a hard line. This had become a sore spot with him.

"He's not a Chief anymore. We're all on an even playing field now. Have you seen him?"

"No. Not since yesterday before we all went to bed. Why?"

Ryan shrugged. "No reason. I was just curious."

Cecilia took a few steps back. It wasn't solid evidence but whatever was bugging Ryan had to do with Chief Rayburn... correction, Mike Rayburn. She'd have to pry it out of him later. If she kept pushing for information, his shortened fuse would make him explode and the last thing she wanted to do was cause a scene in front of everyone.

"I'm sorry. I really can't talk about it right now but trust me. You'll be the first one I tell once I can completely figure it all out."

Ryan walked away from her, and had she had a response to it, he didn't give her a chance to say anything else. She rejoined Ty and her mother, the two of them playing with a toy that Ty had somehow concocted out of some string and some sticks from a tree.

"Can I play?" Sitting beside Ty, she pulled him in for a hug and kissed the top of his head. It was the side where his arm had gotten amputated, and it was still odd to not feel his arm hug her back. She wasn't sure she'd ever get used to the adjustment. She wished she could be as resilient as he was about everything.

"There's one extra action figure right there." Ty pointed at the other literal stick figure. "I'm the good guy, Grandma is the bad guy."

"Well, what does that make me then?" Cecilia picked it up and pretended to make it walk toward them.

"Do you want to be good or bad?" Ty's eyes were bright with excitement. If only they could all be so easily entertained. Cecilia was certain it'd wear off soon and he'd want to go outside.

"I'll be a good guy with you. Sound good?"

"Yep!"

Cecilia kept one eye on Ryan and one eye on her adventures with Ty. It felt as if they were dealing with a good guy, bad guy situation at that very moment in real life, and it didn't involve the looters they had already encountered. Unfortunately, her husband was somehow stuck in the very middle of it all. Ryan wasn't a miracle worker – Cecilia wished he knew that.

❄

Ryan couldn't sit around and wait on the weather. Mike Rayburn hadn't been spotted since the sleet and snow had hit and he worried about what he could be up to. They kept the storage cellar locked but it wasn't as secure as he'd have liked it to be – if there was no one watching, a person could break into it if they wanted it bad enough. And apparently, the looters wanted it, because the danger of them attacking Harper Springs was still relevant. Even if they had moved on to another town, they'd be back – the looting group knew that their little town had a lot to offer and even if it wasn't food or supplies they were after, they'd be back for revenge.

Ryan sifted through his bag of clothes. Throughout his travels between his house and town, as well as to Fox Lake and back, he had gathered clothing from people and out of basements and cellars. Many of the things he had obtained were in various sizes, some too big for him, some smaller, and if he worked it just right, he would be able to layer things to help keep him warm when he went back up to ground level.

He ducked Cecilia's stare. It was no mystery that she was against him going outside but he had to go – if anything, to make sure their storage was okay. He could also get to work on canning some of the vegetables. It was new to him, and he'd make sure to not do them all in case he messed them up. Sitting idle was making him crazy and he also wanted to see if he could spot anyone scoping out the town.

"Where are you going?" Steve grabbed his arm as Ryan approached the stairs, stopping him in his tracks.

"Just gonna go up and check on a few things. Shouldn't be too long."

"Need any help?"

"You'll freeze up there. We don't have any winter clothing to keep you warm enough."

Steve arched his eyebrow, looked up at the door, and back to Ryan. "I can layer clothes like you have. I'm sure someone down here can spare me a few things."

Ryan wasn't in the mood to put up a fight and he also didn't want to seem suspicious in not wanting anyone to go with him. Truthfully, he wanted to be alone, but having Steve with him would at least help if he did get himself in an unexpected bind. He also toyed with telling Steve what his worries were. Cecilia knew some and even that was more than Ryan wanted to give away at the moment. His suspicions were in their early stages and could be nothing at all. The last thing he wanted was everyone running around like crazy, pointing fingers, and making everyone turn against each other. There was no way Harper Springs would survive if that happened.

On second thought, Ryan decided to try and keep Steve from going. After his hesitation in letting his real plan be known, he said, "I'd prefer you stay here and make sure everyone stays safe. I seriously won't be long. I just want to make sure the storage cellar is secure and see what I can gather up to get the canning going. I also want to assess how much snow has fallen and see if I can get a hold of what the atmosphere might be doing."

"Okay, Ryan. I can stay here and make sure things don't get out of hand here. Though I'm sure most of the men down here can hold their own."

"Watch my family for me, okay? They trust you and you've done a great job so far." Ryan winked and forced a smile, hoping to ease the tension some. The more he pushed back, the more Steve dug his heels in and Ryan didn't want to waste any more time. Going halfway up the stairs, he glanced over his shoulder. "I appreciate your help, Steve."

"You got it, buddy. We'll be waiting for you to get back."

Ryan ignored him and went up, the instant chill from the wind nipping at him instantly. Even the layers of clothing he had put on weren't enough to stand up against the bitter cold that swept through the area.

His boots crunched through the snow, and he estimated that there were at least eight inches on the ground so far. Flakes continued to fall from the sky in heavy bands, making the visibility just a few feet in front of him. The clouds were thick and though it was mid-morning, it appeared to be almost nighttime.

Ryan hugged his midsection to keep warm and hurried toward the storage cellar, trying to be quick as he pushed through the howling wind. The temperature was probably in the low teens and with the wind chill, there was no doubt that it was below zero. If he didn't hurry, he'd get frostbite. His face and ears were exposed and those were the areas that were the most vulnerable. The last thing he needed was to lose a body part due to the harsh winter winds.

It felt like the cellar was miles away, though it was only about a quarter of a mile from their shelter. Snow was coming down even heavier now, the flakes so large that it was like Mother

Nature was just dumping buckets of them down on their town. Ryan's clothes were soaked and for a moment, he was willing to admit that going out in it was a mistake. He'd never admit it out loud, but it almost wasn't worth it.

His lungs ached and he coughed – it was dry and unproductive, and it rattled his chest and sent pain down his entire body. His legs were heavy from having to tread through the snow and when he finally caught sight of the storage cellar, he quickened his pace, though it wasn't much of an improvement from how fast he was going before.

His hands shook as he fumbled with the key to the lock. Dropping it, it fell about an inch into the snow and thankfully left a perfect outline, aiding him in finding it. Inserting the key, the lock clicked open, and Ryan hurried inside, shaking off the remnants of snowflakes that covered him completely, leaving a puddle of water at his feet.

Everything was secure as he had expected. Nothing appeared to be moved. His plans to get to canning were hindered – his body ached and all he wanted to do was sit down and rest. Leaning against the wall, his back slid against it until his butt met the floor. Coming to a complete stop, he closed his eyes and took a deep breath, trying to gain his composure.

The sheets they had put over the plants in the pasture were a moot point now. They were buried under the thick snow and wouldn't survive the frigid weather. It took everything Ryan had to not feel completely discouraged and he opened his eyes, scanning the room, making a mental note of their inventory. He needed to get a good idea of what they had in case Mike was up to something, or in case there was another impostor in their group. He was taking Doug's advice – *trust no one.*

After counting everything and doing a double check on the meat they had stored, Ryan attempted to get out of the cellar, but it was complete blizzard conditions. His body would not be able to take another quarter of a mile trek back to the shelter. His skin was numb and that was the first sign of possible frostbite. He'd need to get his body temperature warmed up again before attempting to get back to his family or he'd end up with hypothermia and no way to recover from it.

There was a lantern among some of the supplies and a little propane in the bottle it was connected to. Sifting through a box of random things gathered from a nearby basement, he found a box of matches and lit the lantern, his hands still shaking as he turned the knob to brighten the cellar.

It put off some warmth and he rubbed his hands and got as close to it as possible. Breathing into his palms, Ryan felt the numbness slowly start to fade. His body temperature was warming up, but the heavy layers of clothing were still wet, hindering the process from working as fast as he would like.

He wondered how long it'd take for Steve to want to come to look for him. He had said he wouldn't be gone long but didn't give much of a time frame on when they should start to worry. Ryan decided to give it about fifteen minutes to see how he felt.

He was stuck between allowing his body to recover or letting the snow get deeper and the weather getting worse. If they stayed in the cellars, the winter precipitation would cover the doors to the exits and they'd either have to wait for the temperatures to climb above freezing, or someone would have to continuously clear them off. The worst-case scenario was they'd freeze shut.

He paced, hoping that would get his blood flowing to help warm up. Fifteen minutes – he had to at least wait that long so he wouldn't rush it and end up dead out in the blizzard conditions. It felt like an eternity.

CHAPTER TWELVE

Cecilia passed the time playing with Ty. Darryl and her mom did some reading and sleeping but the mood was standard across the board – everyone had cabin fever and wanted to get some fresh air. She wasn't certain about what the weather was doing. They occasionally could hear the wind howl, but they were deep enough in the ground that it masked the sounds overhead.

The only real indicator she got about current conditions was when one of the men would open the cellar door to make sure it wasn't getting completely blanketed with snow. The last thing they needed was to get trapped inside. They'd do it every thirty minutes and in that short amount of time it had accumulated enough to be significant.

"Mommy, you can play the bad guy this time!" Ty held up one of his homemade toys and handed it to her, his smile so bright that Cecilia longed for a child's innocence. To him, this was one big sleepover and lots of snow meant they'd get to go build snowmen and have snow ice cream. He had only seen large amounts of winter precipitation just a few times in his life, so it was all new to him.

Cecilia continued to go along with Ty's game. Her mind was in a million different directions. She felt the need to watch everyone in the shelter. Ryan's odd behavior had her worried – was everyone out to get each other? Who should she not trust, or would the list of who to trust be shorter?

"You look worried, dear. Want to talk about it?" Margaret sat on the cot behind where Cecilia and Ty were playing, running her fingers down Cecilia's ponytail. Her touch was soothing, and it sent a slight chill down her spine.

"I'm so sick of worrying, Mom." Glancing toward Ty, she handed him his toy. "Mommy has to get up off this floor for a little while, Ty. I think your friend over there might want to play."

Cecilia pointed to another boy he had befriended, and Ty gave no pushback about her wanting to stop. Once he was out of earshot, Cecilia continued.

"Ryan has gone off again. He doesn't even communicate with me. I don't know where he went or when he'll even be back." There was a slight quiver in her voice, and she felt the warmth well up in the corners of her eyes. There would be no stopping the tears that would soon be flowing down her cheeks. And she didn't want to stop them. Maybe one big cry fest was exactly what she needed to get it all out of her system.

"He went to check on the storage. He wanted to make sure it was secure for the weather and from the looters." Steve happened to pass by, stopping when he heard her comment.

Looking up at him, Cecilia nodded and blotted the tears under her eyes with the blanket on her cot. "How long has he been gone? I didn't even see him leave."

Steve pondered her question for a moment, pursing his lips as he thought. "I'd say about thirty minutes ago, but I'm not sure."

"Did he say how long he'd be?"

"No. If he's not back soon we'll go find him." Steve patted

Cecilia on the shoulder. "It's going to be okay. If it's any consolation, each time we look out to clear the snow, it's absolutely beautiful. And we can stop rationing the water for now."

"Thanks, Steve."

Cecilia was about to say something else when she saw the shelter door swing open. She couldn't see his face, but he was covered in snow, his clothes sopping wet as he rested on the top steps. It took him a few seconds to move again, and he edged down the stairs slowly, pulling his hat off. Hurrying toward him, Cecilia took his hand, his skin like ice cubes in her grasp.

"Ryan! Oh my gosh! Someone, get him some blankets!"

Cecilia guided him toward their corner, dodging all the stares from everyone in the shelter. Taking him behind the curtain where the doctor was set up for exams, she helped him out of his clothes. She had tunnel vision, focused only on helping Ryan, and didn't even realize that someone had brought in several blankets that were piled on the makeshift exam table.

Getting her first real glance at Ryan, the sight in front of her made her sick to her stomach. His lips were blue, his teeth were chattering, and the edges of his spiked hair had pieces of ice on them.

"Wrap yourself in these blankets."

Ryan didn't say anything and took a few steps back, sitting on the table. She helped him get wrapped up until the only thing sticking out of the top of the bedding was his head. His vacant expression made her worry that there was some significant damage going on but when Darryl ducked inside the curtain with a cup of steaming hot coffee, Ryan immediately grabbed for it, sticking one hand through an open area of the blankets.

Still shivering, it took him a second to get the cup to his lips and Cecilia also helped in guiding it for him. He was cautious to take a sip but when he did, it was like he couldn't stop himself. His body relaxed as he finished it off and though his body was still shaking, it had calmed down.

"Are you okay, Ryan?" Cecilia asked, cupping the sides of his face in her palms. His skin was still cold to the touch. She worried about frostbite and checked his ears, fingers, and toes, all appeared to be okay. She wasn't a doctor, but he was able to move them around and they weren't discolored.

"I'm fine." It came out in short pants and when Darryl returned with another cup of coffee, Ryan took it as if he hadn't had anything to eat or drink in days. Wrapping his hands around it, this time, he didn't drink it but kept it against his fingers to help regulate his temperature.

"Why did you go out there? You could've died!"

"I didn't..." Ryan trailed off, looking down at the steam that lingered over the top of the cup. "I didn't know it was that bad."

"Is everything okay?"

"Yeah. I marked the cellar with a post so we'd be able to locate it once we can go out there again."

"How deep is the snow?" Cecilia asked, unsure if she wanted to know the answer to it.

"It's hard to know. There were drifts at least fifteen feet high and it is still coming down."

At least Ryan didn't seem to struggle so badly as he talked. He drank the coffee down and put the cup aside, hugging the blankets around him. The ice on his hair and beard had melted and his sopping clothes were piled on the floor.

"I'm glad you made it back."

"I know it's frustrating you, Cecilia. That's not lost on me." His green eyes stared at her, pleading for her to understand why he had done the things he had. Frustration was putting it mildly, and Cecilia had to keep her nagging quiet. He wasn't wandering off to be a nuisance – it was to help and save the people of Harper Springs. She had fallen in love with the man who always did his best for everyone. It was his greatest characteristic and his greatest flaw.

"It's okay, Ryan. I understand why you're doing it. Can I ask one favor of you, though?"

Ryan nodded but didn't say anything.

"Can you please communicate with me better? Tell me where you're going. Tell me when you'll be back. I'm going to worry regardless – there's no sense in hiding it from me."

That made Ryan laugh. "I can do that, babe."

"Oh, and when we have a moment alone, I need you to fill me in more about not trusting people and how you suspect they're up to something. It's like only getting the first half of the movie and it cuts off in mid-sentence. You can't do that to me." She laughed and nudged his shoulder to ease the mood. It was a tough topic that made his grin fade and his brow crease at the subtle mention of the mystery she was trying to debunk.

"Once I get it figured out, you'll be the first to know. Until this weather eases up a bit, the only thing we're gonna be doing is waiting it out. No one needs to go up there right now," Ryan said, pointing upward.

"And the mystery continues." Cecilia kissed his cheek. "I'll go find you some dry clothes. For safe measure, we should have the doctor make sure you're okay." She glanced over her shoulder at him as she pulled the curtain aside. "I love you, Ryan."

"I love you, Cecilia."

❄

GETTING his body back to normal temperature felt like an eternity to Ryan. He stayed rolled up in the blankets, only scooting out of them when the doctor looked him over. There were no obvious signs of hypothermia or frostbite, and he was feeling okay. If he had been out just a little longer, he probably wouldn't have been quite as lucky.

It also helped when Cecilia snuggled up next to him. Sharing body heat with her was the best thing he could do – not only for his physical health but also for his mental health. Having her next to him, taking in the precious time spent with her was a blessing. Even if he needed to be out working the pasture or preparing for more winter weather, it was time well spent.

"You know what we're missing?" Ryan watched Ty and his friend play, his dad read a book, and Margaret napped on the cot near them.

"What's that?" Cecilia asked, clasping her fingers in his.

"A nice roaring fire, hot chocolate, and Christmas decorations."

"That sounds like heaven. Don't forget the turkey roasting in the oven."

Each time they opened the cellar door to clear the snow, Ryan made sure to be at an angle to try and see what the weather was doing. It seemed like they weren't having to remove as much every time but he also wondered if it was wishful thinking.

During their stay in the shelter, it was easy to lose track of time. The sky outside was dark but that wasn't a reliable way to tell what time of day it was. His watch had stopped working during the tornadoes so their only source of having any kind of estimate was the placement of the sun, which couldn't be seen right then.

Sliding off the cot, Ryan stood up and stretched. He had to move to prevent stiff muscles, including his leg which had healed but would never be one hundred percent back to normal after all the damage it had sustained when he had to outrun the coyote.

He spotted Mike Rayburn near the camping shower and bathroom area. His former superior ducked glances with him, avoiding eye contact as much as possible. Ryan debated on whether to talk to him or let it be. The last thing he needed to do was cause a scene and have nowhere to go if people turned on him.

Instead, Ryan circled the cots where everyone was still joined together – some reading, some sleeping, and most sitting around, speculating on the future of Harper Springs and their lives. Having to become nomads wasn't far-fetched and Ryan hoped they could avoid that option at all costs. It'd be an extreme worst-case scenario.

Even when he wasn't looking at Mike, he could feel his eyes on him, burning a hole through him. Though he didn't have absolute proof, Ryan would bet that Mike was up to something just by his current actions toward him. He was likely still pissed that Ryan no longer addressed him as Chief Rayburn, but that resentment would fade – this was more like being secretive or as Cecilia had put it, mysterious. Ryan wondered what he could be up to. His first assumption was working with the looters. What benefit would Mike get from it? He wanted to just blatantly ask him but now wasn't the time.

To many of the townspeople, Mike was still a good guy. He was the beloved fire chief that had saved so many people from wrecks, fires, and accidents. If Ryan confronted him it could turn out ugly for him – he couldn't be positive to think he was on the same playing field as Mike when it came to Harper Springs politics.

"I saw you, Ryan."

Ryan heard Mike break the silence and though the room was full of people chatting, his voice was loud enough. Ryan hurried toward him, bridging the gap between them – if he could get closer, maybe no one would pay any attention to the conversation.

"Saw me where?" Ryan asked, now only a few feet away from Mike. He knew exactly what the other man was referring to but decided to play dumb. Maybe this would go off in a different direction.

"You know." Mike prodded his index finger in Ryan's chest, his glare was so sharp that if looks could kill, Ryan would be dead right where he stood.

"No, I don't, Mike. What in the hell are you talking about?"

Mike smiled, though it wasn't from amusement. He looked like he was going crazy, a sane man losing his mind right in front of Ryan.

"You followed me out to the ranch."

The hair on the back of Ryan's neck stood up and he scoffed. The best thing he could do when he didn't want confrontation was to deny any suspicions that he had followed Mike. If anyone was listening on, maybe they'd believe him. Both men knew the truth and Ryan couldn't think up an explanation as to why he'd follow him.

"I think you're seeing things, Mike. You might want to get some rest." Ryan turned to walk away, sticking to his original plan of not causing a scene in the shelter.

Heat rushed up his arm when Mike's fingers dug into his bicep muscle, turning him back around to face him. His former superior was a bigger man – about three inches taller and at least thirty pounds heavier. Even with size not on his side, Ryan stood strong as Mike stared him down, his jaw clenched, his breathing fast as his grasp tightened around his arm.

"Next time, just tell me you want to go along. You think I'm hiding something?" Mike's voice raised, causing all the muffled conversations around the cellar to fade. Though Ryan couldn't see behind him, he felt every eye of Harper Springs burning a hole in his back.

"Get some rest, Mike. We're all tired. We're all tired of this." Ryan looked him straight in the eye. The man was carrying something on his shoulders – the stress was obvious in his body language and his short temper. "You know you can talk to me. To any of us."

"Let him go, Rayburn." Steve and a few men from the firehouse stood beside Ryan but Mike didn't ease up.

"You should be watching this asshole." Mike poked his finger into Ryan's chest again, his other hand still tight on his bicep. "This has gotten out of hand. I didn't know..." His voice trailed off to a whisper and he let go, freeing Ryan. He appeared to be a man defeated, his emotion exposed like a well-read book.

Mike's last remark was so quiet that Ryan wasn't sure if anyone else had heard it. No one seemed to be indicating that it was out of the ordinary if they had, everyone going back to their conversations, books, and sleep.

Ryan watched Mike disappear into the shower and rather than bring it up with Steve, he left it alone.

"I didn't know..."

He didn't know what, exactly?

CHAPTER THIRTEEN

"Ryan, what was that about?" Darryl cornered him after his altercation with Mike. So much for keeping his concerns a secret. For now, he could play dumb, but people would catch onto the friction happening between the two of them.

Ryan rubbed his arm and watched Mike come out from the showers, ducking past people on the way to his cot. He wasn't speaking to anyone, and most people were staying out of his way. Ryan didn't want to lose sight of him. If there was any trust left between him and Mike, it was completely stripped away with the last few words the man had said that sent red flags sky high with Ryan.

"I don't know what it was about, Dad. Everyone is on edge. We're stuck down here together."

"Cabin fever," Darryl replied, shaking his head. "You two serve on the fire department, right?"

"Did serve on the fire department. I don't think one exists anymore. And if we organize one, the hierarchy of leadership will be different than it was before."

"The last time they opened the doors to clear the snow there was barely a dusting on top. I think the weather might be slowing down a tad," Darryl reported. "I think it might be too late to salvage anything we had to leave behind though."

"We got most of the stuff picked. The plants will be a total loss. And I don't know if what we have is going to be enough to get us through the winter, mainly because I don't know how long winter will last. Spring and summer were abbreviated. Maybe winter will follow suit."

Ryan had lost track of time and was having to estimate what month they were in. Ballpark figure, it was late September, early October, which meant that winter had fired up earlier than ever.

"Is anyone keeping track of what day it is?" Ryan inquired, padding back toward his family's area of the shelter.

"No." Darryl arched his eyebrow and shrugged. "It never occurred to anyone to do it. We all assumed that this would blow over and that would never be an issue."

Ryan pulled the covers down from Ty's face and watched him sleep. It felt like just a few minutes ago, he was playing hard, but sleep made him crash hard and it was probably best for him. Hopefully, he was out before the altercation happened. He didn't need added stress on top of everything he was going through.

Ryan sat beside Cecilia on the cot and closed his eyes. Exhaustion plagued him and physically, he could probably sleep for days. Mentally, his mind wouldn't shut down, hindering him from any chance of getting shut-eye. Neither he nor Cecilia spoke right off, each just allowing the silence to linger. Ryan watched people interact with each other and like clockwork, lanterns burned out and people began to turn in for the night. Only a few lamps burned but it was enough for Ryan to still see Cecilia's face next to him.

"Dad said the snow seems to be tapering off a bit," Ryan whispered. He wanted to talk to her about all his concerns but there wasn't an opportunity to be alone and away from everyone. He was trying to devise a plan for his next steps in investigating what Mike was up to and he wanted her to know, as well as get her opinion on his thoughts. He wanted to make sure he wasn't completely paranoid and reading too much into it.

"That's good. Poor Ty just conked out. One minute he was playing, the next he crawled into bed and was out like a light." Cecilia smiled as she admired their son. "And don't worry. He didn't see what happened between you and Mike." It was as if she had read Ryan's mind and it eased some of the tension in his shoulders.

"That's one person who didn't, at least."

Sighing, he laid back and stared up into the darkness. If he thought hard enough, he could catapult himself back in time and pretend he was lying on their bed, in their house, and he was winding down for the night to prepare for an early day at the mechanic shop the next day. He missed working on cars and tractors. It was a nice escape and troubleshooting the issues was something he always had a knack for. Maybe he could eventually build a car for their use so they could travel farther and quicker than they had been able to with the horses. There were so many tasks and plans he wanted to get done – building or repairing a car would be a crucial one if he could get his hands on the right supplies to get it done.

It'd also help him on his trek to solve the mystery revolving around Mike Rayburn. Sitting up again, he faced Cecilia and took her hands in his, kissing the back of one of hers as he prepared himself to reveal his thoughts on the brewing situation.

"Mike Rayburn is up to no good." He kept his voice low. Though it appeared everyone was sleeping, someone would hear him if he wasn't too careful.

"I kinda got that from the last time you talked to me. Do you have proof? What makes you think that?" Cecilia gulped, her worry palpable as she inquired about his theory.

"I don't have clear and concise proof, no." Ryan ducked his head. "It's just... some of the things he has said aren't normal. They are out of the blue, like he wants to tell us all, but he can't.

It's been driving me crazy... I'm scared I'm just being paranoid and not trusting people. Doug's note had some things that sort of align with Mike also."

"What kind of things are they saying? What did Doug write?"

"Don't trust anyone... things go deeper than what we see... and just now, right in the middle of our tussle, Mike said, I didn't know. He trailed off after that but the look on his face was guilt and fear all wrapped into one."

Cecilia squeezed his hand and looked down at Ty for a few seconds. "What could he be up to? Why would they say things like that?"

"That's what I'm trying to figure out, Cecilia. I haven't been able to sleep. It's consumed my thoughts. Mike has been acting out of character. And Doug... his suicide caught us all off guard."

Doug had said some off-handed remarks about ending it all instead of dying quickly but he seemed to have taken a turn for the better when they had accepted him into Harper Springs. He had the will to want to make it and to work toward rebuilding. And then he shot himself, his suicide hitting them all blindside. Ryan still couldn't get the stain of the other man's blood off his memory, even if the first few weeks of knowing the man were filled with resentment and dislike toward him.

"I think he might be working with the looters." It was the easiest thing to speculate about and though it was a possibility, Ryan's instincts told him it could go deeper than even that.

"You think he's going to help them take us over?" Cecilia's eyes widened and she looked at Ty again, as if her first thought was protecting him. She was a damn good mother and it made it that much easier for Ryan to feel confident enough to leave them when he had to go out and protect their town. She'd make sure to protect their child first over anything else.

"Yeah, partly."

"Partly?"

"I don't know about the rest. Which is why I'm going to go out there and try to trace his steps. Go to his ranch and see where he might be going. He already spotted me following him once so I'm going to have to be a bit more inconspicuous this next time. I'll be better prepared."

"Ryan, the weather is bad. You'll freeze out there."

During their conversation, the whispers had gotten louder, and Ryan put his index finger over his lips to remind both of them to be quieter.

"I'll wear layers. I can make protection for my face and ears out of the hides of the wild boar I killed. I don't plan to be gone long. If the snow really has slowed down, it'll be a day's mission, tops." He was being cautiously optimistic about his plan – trudging through deep snow, dealing with sub-zero temperatures, and having to stay invisible would be a challenge. He could omit all of that from his conversation with Cecilia. Knowing her, she probably was already aware of all the challenges he would face outside of the shelter.

"Are you going to take anyone with you? Steve?"

"No. The less I involve, the better. I don't want to get spotted and I can't trust anyone. You, Dad, your mother, and Ty are about the only ones I can trust right now."

"Steve has helped us so much..."

Ryan cut her off. "No. I don't know much about him. He's helped us tremendously and he's done a hell of a lot for Harper Springs but so did Mike, and now look at where we are. I can't take that chance." He felt guilty for having those feelings toward Steve. They had become friends, but he had to be consistent. If he let his guard down just once, it could be their complete demise.

"So, you trust leaving him here while you're not around to watch us?"

It was a good question that Ryan hadn't thought about. "If he is somehow involved in whatever the hell this all is, and if he doesn't know that we are on to them, everything should be fine.

It's just business as usual. We can tell him I'm out hunting or something."

"Business as usual," Cecilia repeated. "What would you like us to do while you're out there on your mission."

"Weather permitting, I'm planning on leaving first thing in the morning," Ryan replied, looking around the room again. He felt like they were being quiet enough that others weren't hearing. Their cots were far enough away but he also felt like if someone was eavesdropping, it wouldn't be hard to get the main idea of their conversation. "You can start working on the canning. The sooner we can get everything done, the better. We should probably start preserving some of this snow. Bottle it up in the plastic bottles we've been saving. Refill them all."

"So, business as usual," Cecilia said again, smirking.

"Yeah. What's funny about that?"

"Who would've thought bottling up snow in used water bottles was normal? Though it's our way of life now, it just seems funny."

Ryan's lips parted in a smile and a small laugh vibrated in his throat. "Good point, hon. I better try and get some sleep. Maybe my mind will shut down for two seconds."

Cecilia scooted in next to him, the cot too small for both, but neither was willing to let the other go. It was worth the mild discomfort to soak in as much time with her as he could.

Ryan had quoted that it should only take a day to do the digging on Mike Rayburn. His estimate was likely inaccurate but there was no use in fretting over it. Tomorrow was his first step in stopping whatever Mike Rayburn was up to. For Ryan's family and for Harper Springs – the town deserved safety, and Mike was a barrier standing in their way of progressing toward rebuilding and getting their lives on track.

❄

Morning came too soon. Ryan slept a lot more than he thought he would and when he woke up, Cecilia was already helping Ty get ready for the day. He tried to estimate what time it was – with no vantage point and the cellar still dark, there was no way of knowing until he went up to ground level to see.

Whether or not he got to set out on his mission depended solely on the weather. While the snow had stopped falling right before they went to sleep, it could have easily picked back up. Spotting Steve across the room, Ryan slid out of bed and went to him. He hated that he couldn't trust him, and he'd never admit it out loud to the man.

"How's the weather look up there?"

"We just cleared the door. Light snow but nothing like last night," Steve replied. "I'm glad we harvested what we did. Talk about random!" The man smiled, his positive attitude making Ryan feel even worse about developing the attitude he had toward everyone he had been working with.

"Yeah. It's a blessing and a curse all in one."

Ryan stretched out and yawned. He could have easily used a few more hours of sleep. The temperature in the storm shelter was chilly, the drafts from the door being opened keeping it cool. Concerns about winter clothing and bedding were the next milestone they'd have to worry about. They had cotton but it wasn't near enough to make blankets, socks, and sweaters for everyone. At least with everyone together in one small room, the body heat was helping be a natural heater. But how long would that last?

"Steve, I'm going out there today to do more exploring. I'm going to go alone since I don't know what to expect. Hopefully, I can run across more clothes, blankets, and things to keep us warm. If we have more nights like last night, our luck is going to run out. And something tells me, with the pattern we've been dealing with, we're in for a lot worse than that."

"Yeah, considering we had record-breaking heat and massive tornadoes, what's to stop winter from doing the same damn thing?" Steve clicked his tongue on his teeth and shook his head. "You think it's safe to go alone?"

"Gonna have to be. I'd rather you stay here and take care of things. It'll be one less worry on my mind knowing you're here to watch my family and friends. There are a few guys from the firehouse, but Cecilia and Ty seem to have taken a liking to you. And you can help get the canning done. That's going to be one of our top priorities right now."

Ryan quickly shoved aside the warnings from his conscience. Most of what he was saying to Steve was true. Cecilia and Ty had bonded with Steve. And if he had to choose someone to help with his family, it'd be Steve, even if he couldn't trust him completely. He hadn't shown any signs of being on the looter's side but keeping quiet was a decision Ryan had decided to make with everyone, except for letting Cecilia in on it.

The world had shot them off into a different time. The days of worrying about feelings being hurt and coddling people were over. Ryan was doing this for the good of mankind. And as far as he could tell, Steve didn't suspect a damn thing. This was just another one of Ryan's escapades out into the wild. He was on the search for more supplies – he was just choosing to omit the biggest reason he was heading out.

"Yeah, Ryan, we'll take care of everything here. It seems like we're making you do all the dirty work. Past the canning, what else do we have to do? Sit around?"

Ryan patted Steve's arm and laughed. "Steve, my friend, that is the hardest of all. Watching the time pass by with not much to do. Maybe y'all can figure out what we can do with that cotton. And if you happen to hunt anything else, save the fur. It'll all be useful when it comes down to making warm clothes and blankets."

"We'll see what we can come up with." Steve shook his hand. "How long do I need to wait before we go looking for you? Being alone is risky. Too bad you can't pull your cell phone out and give us a call if you need us."

Ryan grinned and glanced at the floor. "I told Cecilia it'd just be today. I don't know how long it'll be, Steve. Three... four days?" Was he overestimating it now? What if he did get into some big trouble and needed them sooner?

"You got it, Ryan. Be safe."

Ryan strode back to Cecilia and Ty. He'd have to say his goodbyes again, leaving them for a third time. He wondered if there would be a day when he wouldn't have to do this anymore but like they had said multiple times, it was like they were back in the old west days, and he was riding off into the sunset.

Ruffling Ty's hair, he sat beside him on the cot. "How'd you sleep, kiddo?"

"Good! It snowed last night!" There was so much light behind the child's eyes. Ryan wished he could be as excited about the wintry precipitation.

"It did! Do you even remember what snow looks like? It hasn't done it much since you've been around."

"I remember! Can I go make a snowman?"

"I don't think you've seen this much snow at once, Ty. I haven't even seen this much snow at once. You'll have to ask your mother if you can. It might be deep enough that you'll disappear." Ryan forced a laugh. It might be deep enough to devour him, too. He dreaded what he'd have to trudge through once he got out there.

"Ask me what?" Cecilia approached them, handing Ty a bowl of steaming oatmeal.

"I wanna play in the snow today!"

"We'll have to see how cold it is out there." Cecilia grabbed Ryan's hand and led him away from Ty. "Still planning to head out today?"

"Yeah. Steve said the snow is light. If I can get going, I might be able to make it back before another blizzard hits."

"How do you know that? It's been so crazy, how can you even begin to forecast something like that?"

"I can't. And if I sit around second-guessing myself, I'm going to waste more time." Ryan leaned in and kissed her cheek. "I'll be safe. Please, don't worry." Telling her not to worry was like telling him not to stress about Mike. "I love you, Cecilia. I'll see you soon."

"I love you too, Ryan."

He ducked her glare. She wasn't meaning it to be so harsh and he couldn't blame her. Just like before, he tried to be empathetic. How would he feel if it was her, running around the area with so much uncertainty happening around them? Cecilia and Ty were his inspiration to come back safely.

He gathered up clothes to put in his bag. After layering so many on his body, there wasn't much left to pack. Losing weight had helped aid Ryan in being able to wear several pairs of pants, most of them fitting over the layer below. He also cut a few squares off his blanket large enough to cover his head and ears. His baseball cap would help hold it on in the wind. If he could keep his head warm, the rest of his body would stay warm with it. He assumed he looked pudgy with the layers, but his appearance didn't matter – if he didn't prepare correctly, frostbite and hypothermia would get him fast. With his one-day estimate a long shot, he had to get ready for days of exposure once he got out and explored.

After saying his goodbyes to his father, Margaret, and Ty, Ryan went up the stairs and out to ground level. Steve was at the storage cellar and a couple of the firemen in his crew were helping him take inventory.

With a quick wave, Ryan went to the small horse barn that one of the men was able to build up before the weather had taken another turn. It wasn't the soundest structure and he feared it had blown over in the harsh winter winds. It had stood up against Mother Nature and he was shocked that the few horses they had left survived the night. It was a rare occasion where luck had worked on his side. Pulling himself up on one, he took it slow, pacing the horse. Riding in the snow was a risk.

He'd make sure to stick close to where he guessed the roads were.

It was probably best not to ride the horse due to the current inclement conditions, but he'd cover far more ground with one. He had to take what he was given at the current moment. For now, Ryan had a horse. Until something else happened along the way, that was all that mattered.

CHAPTER FOURTEEN

Steve watched Ryan ride off, concerned about his friend's safety. He was spooked about something, but Steve wondered why he was so hesitant to let it be known. It was as if a switch had flipped on, and Ryan was paranoid about everything and everyone around him. What had changed? Steve hated that he was missing what Ryan was seeing – was it obvious, or was Ryan just keener to detail? Steve had to chalk it up to Ryan being much more familiar with the area and the people – when a person was acquainted well with another, odd behaviors tended to stick out more. Steve had to tell himself that that was the case and that he just didn't know anyone well enough to make assumptions about out-of-the-blue behavior.

The snow still fell but it was light, lending a very peaceful look to the area. Steve estimated that there was at least a foot of snow on the ground and the drifts were even deeper than that, some over his head against hills and trees. The temperature felt to be hovering right around the freezing mark, but the wind made it feel below freezing.

Without proper clothing, Steve knew his time working outside was limited. He moved fast, salt-curing what was left of the wild hog that Ryan had killed. Keeping it stored in the cool cellar was a good idea, but adding the salt was for safe measure. There was still enough there to feed everyone twice. The best bet would be to shove it all into the snow but the risk of losing it or it getting stolen heightened and Steve didn't want to take that chance. There was also the risk of other animals getting it – there had been an ever-growing amount of wildlife coming up to town, most hungry and thirsty and willing to take a chance getting close to humans.

Steve also gathered the vegetables, so they'd be easier to access for Cecilia. Her plan to put them in jars and run them through a boiling water bath was the best way they could preserve everything before it went bad. They'd have to worry about botulism and food contamination when it was time and the thought of allowing all their vegetables to go bad made Steve sick to his stomach.

"Need some help?" Cecilia stuck her head through the entrance of the storage cellar, making Steve jump.

"Jeez, Cecilia, you scared me! You trekked out here in the snow?"

Grinning, she jumped down inside, landing on her feet without even using the ladder. "Darryl is letting Ty play in the snow right by the entrance to the shelter. Everyone has cabin fever so bad so we're venturing out for a bit. Since it's so cold, I don't think we'll be out long since none of us have winter clothes."

"Yeah, and it's pretty cold out there. The last thing we need is for all of us to get sick. There are not enough medical supplies to handle that."

"Everyone grabbed their blankets from their cots." Cecilia's brow creased and she looked at the dirt floor, kicking up some dust with her boot. "I wish I could think up a good way to make some warmer clothing. We didn't produce enough cotton and we don't have the equipment to concoct something anyway."

"We have the hides from the boars. We could try and do

something with that. I'm not a major hunter but I'm sure someone here is."

"Oh, yeah. Big hunting area around here," Cecilia confirmed with a shake of her head. "But that's not enough. Maybe we can send a couple of guys on a hunting trip. Deer, boar, fox, and even mountain lions. We could do like the Native Americans did and use up every bit of the animal we can."

"As long as they're a good shot. We can't use up too much ammunition in case the looters come back," Steve replied, piling up the vegetables in a tote.

"Always something to think about," Cecilia sighed. "It's so crazy how we took life for granted before everything. If we were cold, we had a sweater. If we wanted to hunt, we grabbed a box of shells. There was no worry about replenishing anything – we always bitched about small paychecks and not having any money but in the grand scheme of things, it was all a bunch of sound and noise. Life was great."

"And it will be again." Steve patted her on the shoulder. "We're stronger because of all this."

"Do you think Ryan will make it back this time?" It was a drastic change in subject but evidently, something that Cecilia had on her mind and needed to talk about.

"Of course, I do. You don't?"

She bit her bottom lip and ran her hand over an ear of corn. "I swear he has more lives than a damn cat."

"Which is all the more reason to believe he'll get back here safely."

"The problem is, I don't know how many he has left." A tear trickled down her cheek and she quickly wiped it away. "I'm so sick of belly aching over this. We need to get down to business. It's cold in here and my toes are already going numb. What do you need me to do?"

Steve knew she wasn't done talking about it, but he didn't want to press the matter. They did have work to do so he let it be until there was a more opportune time to talk. Cecilia and

Mindy had bonded. Maybe she'd completely open up to her and feel better once she vented.

Forcing a smile, Steve lifted the tote. "I guess we can get to canning. There's some propane bottles in the back and a couple of camping stoves. Those Mason jars you gathered from your folk's cellar are also down here. Ryan made sure they didn't get destroyed. We can also refill some of the water bottles and canteens with the snow. Cold water sounds amazing right now."

"Then let's get to it."

Cecilia grinned and began gathering the supplies she needed to get the canning done. It was going to be a long, cold day, but to Steve, it was better than sitting around the shelter wasting time. At least the camping stoves would put off a little warmth. And at least he'd feel productive about something.

❄

RYAN WASN'T sure where Mike Rayburn was, but his first course of action would be to go back to his ranch and see if he could rustle up some kind of clue to move his speculation in the right direction. The wind bit him to the bone despite the layers of shirts and jeans he was wearing. The blanket made into a beanie was helping and doing better than not having something covering his head, but he wouldn't be able to do long hours out in the weather. He couldn't risk getting sick or losing a finger or toe.

He kept the pace slow. There were areas in the snow that the horse slid and almost fell in, so keeping it close to where the original highways and roads were was a safe way to make sure they'd stay on solid ground if they happened to fall into a deep pit of snow. At times it was hard to remember where the roads were – it had been months since Ryan had driven the roads and though he had been in the area most of his life, his memory was fading when it came to details like that. Now his compass was on, wanting him to go the most direct route to his destination but he couldn't risk losing the horse. He'd be able to cover triple the ground with it as opposed to tiring himself out much faster on foot.

He had also debated on whether going alone was a good idea. His overreaction to not trusting anyone might have been harsh. Steve was a good man that Ryan felt almost certainly wasn't a part of whatever might be going on. He would have enjoyed his friend's company on their ride to investigate, but on the other hand, he also needed Steve back in Harper Springs to take care of his family and get the ball rolling on the winter preparations.

Steve was from Oklahoma where they had harder winters than their part of Texas. He also knew about quick harvesting when the weather turned bad. His expertise in those areas made him the best candidate to stay back and supervise everything on their checklist. And since he could trust him, he knew his family was going to be okay without him there to make sure.

The ride alone made Ryan's thoughts run wild. The most plausible thing he could think of with Mike was that he was working with the looters. He hoped it would be as simple as that, though being an inside source for the growing group of thieves could be detrimental. He wouldn't be able to stomach the idea of giving up their town to those people after all the hard work they had put in. But at the same time, he wondered if it was worth fighting over. The town itself wouldn't be that bad of a loss – with the harsh weather going from extreme to extreme, leaving the area could be a good idea if they had the resources to locate it. It was the loss of food and supplies that made Ryan's defense mode turn on full force. They had worked hard gathering and growing what they had – He couldn't just let someone march in and take it without a big fight.

Hopefully, figuring out what Mike Rayburn was up to might put a hitch in their plan if that's really what he was up to. What else could he be doing? The world was different now – their options were completely limited to just surviving.

Ryan pondered several possibilities during his ride in hopes to keep his mind off the bitter cold that nipped at every inch of his body. Looters were the top reason on his list. Or what if Mike was working with some kind of higher power? What if the government was responsible for what was going on? It was completely far-fetched, and Ryan had never been a conspiracy theorist, but as crazy as things had escalated, he couldn't downplay anything.

What would the conspiracy be? Wipe out areas for population control? Warfare against the United States? With the Middle East waging war against America, what if they finally found a way to kill them and completely cripple any chance at coming back stronger? Ryan had read studies where it was believed that the government had ways to manipulate the weather. What if this was one of those instances?

Ryan shivered, partly due to the icy cold weather, and partly out of fear of the unknown. Hopefully, this was all just his imagination running wild due to not having anyone to talk to. He'd stick to his first worry – warding off looters who were using Mike as an inside source. He'd much rather take that on than weather manipulation or possible war being controlled by the atmosphere.

He came up on Mike Rayburn's ranch, the hill where his house once stood off in the distance. The mangled trees surrounded the concrete foundation, reminding him of what it once was – a beautiful, two-story farmhouse that was the epitome of a blue-collar family doing well in America.

Ryan eased the horse into the valley, its hooves skidding on the icy surface below. In weather like this, it would be very easy for someone to be a tracker – if someone was following Ryan there would be no issue in knowing exactly where he was, but he didn't have a choice. There wasn't enough time to cover up his tracks. If they continued to let whatever was happening pan out, they were down to months and possibly even weeks when it came to survival.

He had to keep watch in three places – behind him for trackers, in front of him to make sure Mike wasn't there, and down, to make sure that the horse wasn't going to step into deep snow and break its leg. The last thing he needed was to have an injured horse and even worse, to have to put the animal out of its misery.

Being able to see tracks in the snow would also help Ryan. Clean and fresh snow meant he would be alone. Though it was still snowing, it wasn't falling fast enough to fill in anyone else's tracks, at least, not yet. He continued to shiver and wondered if the temperature was dipping even more than when he left town. He had to chalk part of it up to his imagination – with the gloomy skies, steady snowfall, and occasional wind gusts, it was enough to play with anyone's mind.

Approaching the area where Ryan estimated the cellar was, he slid off the horse, guided it through a moderate-sized snow drift, and tied it to a tree nearby. Hugging the layer of clothes around his midsection, he looked for something to try and help clear off the snow so he could find the door to the cellar. It was about the only place he might be able to find something that Mike Rayburn could be hiding.

Ambling back through the snow to the dead tree, he pulled on a tree branch, the wood snapping and finally giving way with added force. The heavy snow that had accumulated on the branches helped, the weight proving to be too much for the tree that seemed to have either been killed during the tornadoes or burned up during the drought – regardless of its demise, it was a win for Ryan, and it was the perfect size to use to push the snow around on the ground.

It was hard to get a good vantage point of where the cellar might be. He tried to think about before the weather had turned on them, back to when everyone at the firehouse would join for barbecues and parties. There was a large, in-ground swimming pool behind the house and the cellar was about two hundred yards from the house in the side yard, up next to a row of pecan trees that Mike was so proud of, now most mangled up, twisted, and uprooted.

Ryan took large steps, roughly estimating the measurement with his stride. Clutching the tree branch, his hands ached as he tightened his grip, the cold air harsh against his exposed skin – unfortunately, he was unable to cover his entire body with the lack of winter clothes and supplies they had back in town.

Lowering the branch, he swept it from side to side like a broom, pushing snow sideways, the powdery substance blowing in the wind. He hit hard layers and kicked them with his boot, trying to knock the ice layers under the snow loose. It took a lot of energy and time but if he couldn't find the cellar, his entire trip out to the Rayburn ranch was a complete waste of time and resources.

With his next step, Ryan felt like he hit a hollow spot. Stomping his boot, it felt much different than the ground just a few feet behind him, so he focused there, working harder to clear the deep snow that swirled on the ground. Once he got about six inches swept away, he was faced with another icy layer. Remembering he had a hammer in his bag, he pulled it out and slammed it against the sub-zero layer that was serving as the perfect force field to keep him out of Mike Rayburn's property.

He had to take a break often – his lungs burned and ached from breathing in the cold, dry air. When he coughed, his chest tightened, and he tried to pay attention to any signs of hypothermia or frostbite. Checking his hands, they looked to still have some color in them. He had a thin pair of gloves on, but they were now wet, chapping his skin and damaging it.

Each time he took a break, he had to force himself to keep working. He could see the door of the cellar right under the ice, the translucency giving him enough of a clue that he was in the right spot. If he could just get the ice layer broken, he'd be able to get in and start digging for clues. He had to stop with the self-doubting – Mike was up to something, and Ryan wasn't going to allow his mind to convince him otherwise.

With one more hard hit, the ice cracked like a piece of glass, the split spreading enough for Ryan to remove what was left with his hands. Right below him was a haven to get out of the wind and snow – but most importantly, his chance to hopefully get down to the bottom of what his former friend and Chief was up to.

CHAPTER FIFTEEN

Cecilia set up the camp stoves – there was two total, which meant she had eight burners to work with. The large pots they had found took up two burners each which was fine – it was going to take two burners to help warm up the water hot enough to get the canning jars to seal.

Mindy helped her stuff the jars with vegetables and fill each with water. Steve was cutting them up small enough so they would fit, and Ty was busy playing with the clippings that they wouldn't be able to use.

"That sure is keeping him occupied," Mindy said, motioning toward Ty with the end of a carrot.

"He's helping!" Cecilia replied, smirking. "I love how it doesn't take much to keep him busy. I'm glad he doesn't have ADHD or something. This would be hell for everyone involved if he did. I'm so glad he has a great imagination."

"So, where is that husband of yours?"

Mindy's tone came off harsh and Cecilia had to tell herself that she didn't mean it. It was almost accusatory like he wasn't around helping them. If only she could spout off what he was up to, namely saving their asses from whatever or whoever was causing the turmoil, it would help alleviate the tension in her mind and the weight she was carrying on her shoulders. But she couldn't spill it – it could compromise everyone's safety. Not being able to trust anyone felt like Cecilia was going into battle with her hands tied behind her back.

"He went out to see if there were any supplies he could gather. Also, to hunt – we could use animal hides now more than ever." Keeping her replies to a minimum would be the best – she felt like she had an arrow pointed over her head, telling everyone she was covering for Ryan. In reality, it was just paranoia.

"He's brave for going out in this. Looked like more snow was on the way from the north." Mindy stuffed a jar full of potatoes and screwed the gold metal ring around the top of the jar, handing it to Cecilia.

Lowering it into the boiling water, Cecilia made sure they didn't overload the two pots so they wouldn't spill over. The water was at a rolling boil, perfect to get them sealed up as best as they could. It still wouldn't do the job of a pressure cooker, but it was better than leaving them in storage to rot. This would preserve them a little longer but probably not long enough to get them through to planting season again.

"How bad did it look?" Cecilia asked, a knot forming in her stomach. Ryan had already been caught in the middle of the first blizzard that came through. And this time, he was a lot farther away from home.

"Just dark and ominous. I've been to a lot of places, and I know what an incoming winter storm looks like. How long was he planning on staying out there?"

Cecilia dipped the metal tongs into the water bath and checked the bottles. She'd need to leave them in longer – the band wasn't sealing around the jars quite yet.

"I think he planned to come back this evening."

"I hope so, or even sooner than that. How much experience do you guys have with snow around here?"

Steve joined in on the conversation, his smile usually infectious, but this time, Cecilia couldn't get her mouth to move that way. "I have quite a bit. Oklahoma gets a lot more snow than Texas. And long spans without electricity aren't far off either, so while this completely sucks, it's happened before to me."

"Only help was there to fix it. It wasn't long-term," Mindy chimed in, handing another jar to Cecilia.

"No, not long term like this, but we had spans of several weeks where we didn't have running water, electricity, heaters, or anything."

Cecilia listened to Mindy and Steve banter back and forth, keeping one eye on the boiling water and one eye on Ty who continued to play with the pieces of vegetables they had tossed on the floor. What they didn't throw away or can, they could use to lure in rabbits and rodents. For now, it was helping entertain Ty. The less he asked about Ryan and the more he focused on other things, the better it was for Cecilia to not have to explain anything. She couldn't even tell her son the real reason his father was out there, running around the frozen tundra. He wouldn't understand it and she couldn't risk someone hearing her.

"Cecilia?"

Looking up, she saw both Steve and Mindy staring at her. Her cheeks heated up and she didn't want to admit that she had zoned out and didn't even hear what they were saying.

"Yeah?"

"How long do we need to keep the jars in the water bath?" Mindy's eyes widened but she looked sympathetic.

"Another ten minutes and we'll see if they finally sealed up."

Mindy patted her arm and grinned. "Honey, if you aren't up for this, we can take care of it. Do you need to go rest?"

"No, I'm okay. I can't sit around and not do anything. It makes me think too much."

"I understand. But if you need to, you can go back to the shelter. Steve and I can take care of it all."

"You're very kind but I'm good. How many jars do we have left?"

Mindy counted the boxes. "Looks like twenty-five jars."

"Good. We have plenty. I wish we had enough vegetables to fill every one of them." Cecilia squeezed the tongs, clanking the metal against the side of the camping stove. If she went back to the shelter now, she'd drive herself crazy worrying about Ryan. At least right now, she could channel her nervous energy on something productive. After everything he was doing for the people of Harper Springs, it was the least she could do for her husband.

❄

EVEN THOUGH RYAN knew no one was there by the lack of tracks in the snow, he was still cautious as he went down the steps into the shelter. He wasn't quite sure where Mike was, and he possibly could have come back to his ranch before the heaviest of the snow hit and was hiding down inside.

Grabbing a flashlight from his belt, Ryan flicked it on and checked every corner of the small room. Breathing heavily, he could see the stream of breath come out of his mouth – it was probably just as cold down in the cellar as it was above, but at least the wind wasn't blowing and that helped ease the chill to his bones.

It didn't appear that anyone was there. Keeping the flashlight up, he looked around. There were boxes stacked up on the far wall and a wine rack adjacent to it. Ryan pulled a bottle from it and dusted off the label. It was a chardonnay that had been bottled about five years before at a winery in Lubbock. And luck was on his side – it was a screw cap so he wouldn't have to mess with a cork.

Taking his gloves off, he opened the wine and sniffed it. It had been forever since he had a drink of any type of alcohol and his mouth watered at the thought of out it'd taste. He'd have to be careful and not overdo it. Since it had been so long, any amount would be a shock to his system and make him feel buzzed a lot quicker than when he drank more often.

Taking a sip, the dryness of the wine was strong, and it burned worse than Ryan had anticipated. It was almost like he was drinking a shot of whiskey, but the warmth effect worked wonders on getting his body temperature to level out. The warm fuzzy feeling flowed down to his stomach. Taking another sip for good measure, he screwed the cap back on and set it on a nearby shelf. If he drank any more, he'd feel it, and he needed to be on his game in case Mike showed up – and hopefully in case he ran across some information he'd have to decipher.

Pulling a box from the wall, he opened it up, blowing to get some of the dust from it. It burned his nose and he sneezed. It was almost an invasion of privacy going through Mike's belongings like he was. He second-guessed himself again – what if he was reading way too far into all of this and Mike wasn't up to a damn thing? How would he feel if someone had a hunch about him and he found them rifling through his stuff? How would he approach the person? Ryan considered backing away, but his gut instinct told him otherwise. He had to get to the bottom of this, even if his gut reaction wasn't justified. At least it would clear Mike of all suspicion and ease the tension a tad.

The first box was just full of family photo albums and heirlooms. Ryan was careful with those things – they seemed timeless and even though Mike might have been playing against Harper Springs, Ryan felt the need to respect the belongings.

Moving that box aside, he grabbed another. It was Christmas decorations. Feeling the need to go through it all, just in case Mike had hidden something, Ryan checked everything down to the bottom before putting it all back in its place.

There were only a few boxes left and Ryan was feeling discouraged. Maybe Mike was smart enough to not hide anything top secret here. Continuing the search, the third box had more decorations and patio items. Scooting it aside, Ryan grabbed the bottle of chardonnay again and took another sip. It wasn't that it tasted good but the warmth that flowed down his esophagus to his stomach made him stop shivering and for the first time since he set out on this trek, everything began to normalize.

Sitting on the floor, he leaned back against the dirt wall. Everything around him – a far table, shelves, the wine rack, and the boxes were all completely covered in dust. There were spider webs when he flashed the light up toward the ceiling. He wondered how many black widows and scorpions had made this place their home. If it was anything like the cellar back on his property, Mike probably had to spray at least twice a year like Ryan had to.

He scoffed at his random thoughts – it was like someone had a remote control that took hold of his brain and made him switch from Mike's possible conspiracy to exterminating bugs in a cellar. It was probably also the wine helping, and though it had been months since Ryan had a drink, it was crazy how much his body had adjusted and wasn't as tolerant to it as before.

He slid the rest of the chardonnay into his bag and went ahead and grabbed two more off the rack. Cecilia would think he was insane for doing it, but she'd also love it when he poured her a glass. Since he wasn't bringing any intel back, at least he wouldn't be empty-handed. It'd be his and her secret and though he wanted to take more, he couldn't do too much, or Mike would notice the gap in the wine rack.

Flashing the light around the cellar again, Ryan stopped the light when he saw a small ledge about ten inches below the top near the ceiling. It was wooden and looked like Mike had added it in as an afterthought. It was high up and out of Ryan's reach. Standing, he looked around for something that would be tall enough to get him up there. There was no ladder or step stool but there was a filing cabinet that would hopefully be close enough to give him the added height needed to get to it.

Steadying himself, Ryan pulled up on it, attempting to keep his balance. The filing cabinet was full, so his weight made it sway slightly and he stopped, his knees bent as he stood on top of it. It felt like he was on a boat in choppy water, but once everything balanced out, he straightened his posture, reaching toward whatever was on the small ledge that was serving as a hiding spot.

It was metal and cold, and Ryan's heart skipped a beat as if he had just stumbled on a lost treasure. Sliding it off the wooden ledge, he brought it to eye level. It had a small luggage lock on it and was about ten inches by thirteen inches. Something inside slid around as Ryan jumped off the filing cabinet, hitting the floor below him with a hard thud. A cloud of dust kicked up around him and he backpedaled toward the corner where he had recently sat, next to the wine rack and storage boxes he had sifted through.

Pulling the hammer out of his bag, Ryan hit the lock several times. For a luggage lock, it stood strong, and he tried again, the clank of the hammer against the metal box loud, echoing against the walls around him. With one more try, the lock finally fell apart, granting him access to whatever might be inside the box.

Opening the lid, he expected the contents to be dusty, matching everything else he had come across in the cellar. But what he saw inside was pristine – there was a spiral notebook, a compass, a small flash drive, and a cell phone. Ryan tried to turn it on but just like everyone's, it was dead. Flipping the spiral open, the inside of his mouth grew dry when he read the title on the very first page.

Atmospheric Frequency Control Project

Ryan's assumptions had to be right. Atmospheric control? But who was heading this? Mike certainly didn't have the means to do it, so he couldn't be working alone.

Flipping to the next page, Ryan felt like he was reading a novel that he couldn't put down. He had to skim fast – his sudden wave of paranoia was stronger than any bout he had felt before he found the spiral with notes jotted all over the pages. It was a government project in the works to use as warfare. Bile gathered in the back of Ryan's throat. Was he reading this all correctly? How could that even be possible?

Turning the page, he tried to read as much as he could. If he took the journal with him, that would send Mike into a tailspin once he got back to take more notes or investigate it. But at the same time, Ryan wanted him to know that his secret was out. But what was Mike's capacity in all of this? What was he gaining by working with the government on manipulating weather for war? And if it was the US government, why were they killing off their own people? If it was the US government. The spiral notebook hadn't specified if it was the US, which opened up even more speculation for Ryan.

"Well, well, well..."

The voice pulled Ryan from the notebook and when he looked up, heat coursed through him, hot enough to melt all the snow and ice that the recent storm had dropped on the area. Scooting, he tried to stand up but Mike pointed a gun at him, halting him from doing anything. Dropping the notebook, Ryan held his hands up to show he wasn't going to make a move, his heart thumping so hard that he was certain Mike could see it through all the layers of clothes he was wearing.

"Taking in some good reading, Ryan?"

Ryan stared down the barrel of the gun, knowing any second the man standing over him could pull the trigger and kill any chance of his family's survival. For now, he had to play it cool. But how would he be able to talk himself out of this? Mike had caught him red-handed. How could he have let his guard down? He wasn't expecting to stumble across something so big so fast.

"It's interesting, yeah."

"You know I have to kill you now, right?" Mike trained the gun on him, taking a few steps closer. If he pulled the trigger at that very second, it'd hit Ryan right between the eyes.

"No, you don't." Attempting to keep his voice steady, Ryan felt it shake, hindering any chance of not appearing nervous.

"Why is that? You've seen what I've been up to."

"Because I'm here to help."

"You're a damn liar, Ryan. How in the hell do you think you'll help?"

Ryan thought for a second, the cellar growing eerily quiet. "We can stop this. Try and get everything back to normal."

Mike shook his head and moved the gun up and down. "Hell no! It goes way beyond anything you can imagine. You're gonna come with me. I'm gonna show you exactly what is going on. And then..." He held the index finger of his free hand up and pointed it at Ryan. "...And then I'm going to dust your ass. What you know is too much and I can't have anyone else knowing about it. Only the people involved."

"Who is involved?" Ryan asked.

"That's why I'm taking you there. You'll know soon enough. But it won't matter. You're a dead man walking. I just want you to see why this is going on. You've been the one asking the most questions. Now you'll know."

"Don't do anything stupid, Mike. Let me go. If it's bigger than I can imagine, how in the hell am I going to do anything? Let me get back to my family and we'll pretend like this didn't even happen." Leveling with Mike wasn't working. Ryan needed to tread with caution. The look in Mike's eyes showed insanity – one wrong word would take away any chance Ryan had of getting out of this alive.

"Stop talking, Ryan, and stand up!" Mike motioned the gun upward. "Don't make any sudden movements or I will shoot you. And if you say another word, I'll shoot you."

Ryan fought everything inside himself to not speak. Standing, he clutched the handle of his bag and waited for Mike's next command. He had to come up with a plan to get away. Where was this Atmospheric Frequency Control Project? And how long would it take someone from Harper Springs to realize something was wrong?

Ryan wasn't exactly clear about when he'd be back in town. And suddenly, he regretted not being more open to Steve about what he was really up to. It would be as if he had fallen into a black hole, simply disappearing with no way to track him down.

CHAPTER SIXTEEN

Steve spent the remainder of the day canning the vegetables they had harvested. The weather had cooperated for the most part, and only about two more inches had fallen, adding to the foot that was already on the ground. Organizing the jars, he tried to keep everything similar together on the shelves in their storage cellar.

Cecilia had been a great help and though she occasionally had to go check on Ty, she and Mindy had completed most of the hard work, though both would argue, and staying close to the boiling pot was great to keep warm.

"You coming back to the shelter?"

Cecilia broke his thoughts, and he glanced over his shoulder at her. The poor woman looked exhausted – mainly from worry for her husband and son. He was glad she had Mindy to talk to from a woman's perspective. He understood why Ryan went out on excursions. He hated that he wasn't there with him this time.

"Here in a bit. I was going to see if I could do a little hunting before it got too dark. With all the wildlife coming up, I might get lucky."

Cecilia nodded and tucked a strand of hair behind her ear. "Maybe Ryan will be back soon."

"Maybe." Steve shook his head and grabbed two cans of corn from the shelf, handing them to her. "How about you take that back and cook it up? It's just corn but it'll be a nice change of pace from everything else. Does Ty like corn?"

"He does. One of the few vegetables I could ever get him to eat." Cecilia hesitated. "Are you sure? I don't want to run through all this too fast. It's going to be a long winter."

"I'm sure. We didn't plant and harvest it just to stare at it on a shelf." Steve patted her arm. "Ryan is okay, Cecilia. He'll make it back."

"I don't know, Steve. Something feels different this time."

She acted like she wanted to say more but stopped herself. Opening her mouth to speak, she looked down at the floor and edged toward the steps, taking the first two up before stopping again.

"You know you can talk to me, Cecilia." Steve stayed toward the back of the cellar, not wanting to make her feel uncomfortable.

She shook her head and bit her bottom lip, hoisting the jars of corn in each hand. "Nah, it's nothing, Steve. We got a lot done today. It's nice to put in a good day's work."

"It'll be even better if I can kill a couple of rabbits or something. Would be nice to have some meat with that corn."

"Yeah, I'll take this back and hold off for a bit just in case you do get something. Thanks, again, Steve. I better go check on Ty. He's probably starving."

She didn't let Steve reply before going up the stairs, the cellar door slamming behind her. Steve looked upward for a few seconds, half expecting her to come back down and spill whatever it was on her mind, but she didn't. Turning back to the jars of vegetables, he finished organizing them and taking inventory, mentally noting that he had given her two jars. He wanted to keep an eye on their supply – they did lock the storage cellar, but it wasn't exactly top-notch security. If a looter or drifter wanted in bad enough, it wouldn't be a big challenge for them.

Pulling his rifle from the corner, he checked to make sure it was loaded. He had spotted a few rabbits just north of town near the river. Hunting wasn't his strong suit, but his mouth watered at the thought of roasting one over a fire. Propane usage was a concern – the surplus they were lucky to have was running low and they had used up quite a bit doing the canning. If the weather allowed, they'd do a lot of their cooking over an open flame. They'd reserve the propane and camping stoves for when they were stuck inside, and everything was too wet to burn.

After making sure everything was organized to his liking, Steve went up the stairs to ground level and locked up the cellar. He needed to mark where the cellar was just in case more snow came through, but he didn't want it to be obvious to outsiders. There was a metal t-post leaning against a tree and he slid it down into the snow – the ground was wet enough that it went right in without much effort. It seemed obvious to him but maybe not to everyone – it could just be a random post sticking out of the ground. It was too hard to find the cellar before and they couldn't risk losing sight of it in the middle of another snowstorm.

Gripping the rifle, he trudged through the snow. His legs were heavy as they sank deep into the cold, his muscles tightening as he lifted them to keep moving. The sun was beginning to set, and he had to move fast. Snow was falling again, a tad heavier than it was just a few hours ago. His thin clothing was layered but still not heavy enough to protect him for extended amounts of time outside.

The moon was showing through the clouds, the silver silhouette beautiful, like Steve was in the middle of a picture on a Christmas card. He had to think that way or he'd lose his mind – his body shivered, his teeth chattered, and he debated on just heading back to the shelter before he got stranded. The thought of warm, lean meat to accompany the fresh vegetables they had worked on inspired him to keep moving, despite his body's warnings to go back to a warm place.

Nearing the river, he tried to find a spot to hide. He stuck out like a sore thumb – his black clothes were obvious against the sparkling white of the snow that spread throughout the area. Edging toward the riverbank, he noticed chunks of ice on top of the water. It wasn't completely frozen – the motion of the water had helped hinder that, but it was close to being solid.

He heard something rustle behind him and turned on his heel, his mind resorting to the possibility that it could be another person. Crouching low, he scooted toward what was left of a tree, hiding behind the trunk. Gripping the rifle, he aimed it outward, scanning for whatever it could be. He couldn't be trigger-happy – what if it was someone from Harper Springs? Even if it wasn't, would he be able to pull the trigger to save his life? He'd never been put in a situation like that to truly know.

The snow crackled again, and Steve squinted – despite the overcast weather, the moon was reflecting off of the snow, the white bright enough to make him not be able to see well.

And then he saw it – a ten-point buck just on the edge of some trees. Steve's heart raced, his palms were clammy, and he froze where he was. A deer could feed them for God knew how long. And they could use the hide for winter clothing.

Resting the rifle on his shoulder, he aimed. If he waited much longer the animal would saunter off and out of range for him to be able to kill him. Resting his index finger on the trigger, Steve steadied himself, attempting to calm his nerves. If he pulled the trigger and wasn't ready, it'd be a miss, ensuring the buck would be gone and he'd miss his chance. He also had to make sure that the shot he took would be fatal – he didn't want the animal running off with a wound that would make him suffer.

Taking a deep breath, Steve continued to watch. The animal was oblivious to the fact that a gun was trained on him. He had a hard time walking in the snow, his skinny legs fighting against the ice. Finally feeling confident enough to take a shot, Steve tightened his finger, the gunshot ringing out so loud that it echoed against the hills.

When he opened his eyes, he expected to see the deer gone with nothing to take back to town. He was wrong. Pulling himself to a standing position, Steve slowly walked toward his kill, the buck dead on the top layer of snow. There was minimal blood, which meant the shot killed him almost instantly.

Kneeling, Steve lifted the buck's head, his dark black eyes still open, staring up at the night sky. He was a big deer which meant that getting him back to Harper Springs was going to be hard. The slick layer of snow would help until he reached areas where it wasn't as packed. He wasn't far from Harper Springs. Maybe he could hurry and get some help, but he wasn't confident in leaving it unattended – other animals lurked, ready to pounce on anything to eat and it was the same for the looters. Though they couldn't see them constantly, they were hiding out, watching their every move for an opportunity to take something.

Steve would estimate that the buck probably weighed around one hundred and thirty to one hundred and fifty pounds. If he could stay on solid snow, he could probably drag it back. He'd have to try, or at least get it as close as he could before needing help.

Grabbing the deer's back legs, he held each one on either side of his hips and pulled. The animal's dead weight proved harder to move than he had anticipated. Steve's feet dug deep into the snow with each attempt to pull, making the deer feel about fifty pounds heavier than he was. Gritting his teeth, he pressed on, unwilling to give up his kill.

He had gone about one hundred feet when he decided to rest. The cold air was burning his lungs and his body ached. Bending at the waist, Steve coughed – it was dry and unproductive, another gift from the cold winter air.

Standing up again, he looked toward where he had shot the deer. It didn't feel like they had moved that far and if he stayed at his current pace, it'd take him until morning to get back. Glancing at the dead animal and back up, his heart skipped a beat when he thought he saw someone looking at him from behind a tree. It had to be his imagination – he was paranoid of someone watching him and it was just his mind playing tricks on him.

Only, he saw it again, and this time, the man held eye contact with him for at least five seconds before disappearing behind the tree again. Steve toyed with the idea of confronting them. His ammunition was low and he didn't want to risk something happening. Right now, his main goal was to get the deer back to town. But who was the person? Were the looters attempting to make a move on them again?

Gripping the legs of the deer again, he checked one more time to see if he was being watched. There was no one there and though it was definite that he had spotted someone, he had to tell himself that it was his imagination. Whoever it was knew he had made a big kill, which meant that Harper Springs was possibly in danger of the looters making a move on their supply.

He had to hurry and get back, to preserve the deer and to let the other men know. He also wanted to see if Ryan had made it back yet. Something bigger than gathering supplies was going on with him and Cecilia was on the verge to tell it all. There was too much uncertainty to be out alone. They needed to work in teams to ensure safety.

Though an attack wasn't certain, they had to be ready just in case. Steve delved deep to find energy – he couldn't stop again until he was back in town. His adrenaline pumped, giving him what he needed to move fast and pull his kill home. The next step was prepping for battle. They might not make their move within the next few days, but it would come eventually. The more they prepared, the better off they would be.

❄

THE ROPE TIGHTENED around Ryan's wrists, digging into his skin. The burning sensation shot up his arms. He considered attacking Mike. As he tied Ryan up, he wasn't holding the gun.

Ryan could jump at him and tackle him, taking over whatever plan Mike was up to. But Mike outweighed Ryan but at least fifty pounds. Would Ryan be able to overtake him, or would it just piss Mike off more?

He had to try – if he allowed Mike to kidnap him, he could kiss his family goodbye. At least he could go down trying. Right now, the only thing tied up was his right wrist. Mike moved to the left and before he could knot the rope, Ryan lunged at him, hugging Mike's midsection as if he were a linebacker on the line.

As predicted, Mike was strong, and Ryan grunted as he struggled to get the other man down. They both fell to the floor with a loud thud and Ryan's head hit something. For a second, his vision went black, and he fought through it. If he gave up now, it'd just make things worse. He had committed to trying to fight his way free from Mike and he couldn't succumb to weakness.

Both men struggled on the floor and Ryan kept one eye on the gun that Mike had left sitting on a table near them. He had already stripped Ryan of all his weapons and though there were several guns, the one Mike had trained on him was the closest to get to.

Pinning Mike to the floor, Ryan made a move to go for the gun. It would mean letting go of Mike and it was a hard feat to get him down but that didn't matter – the only way he'd be able to defeat him is if he got the gun first. In a physical battle, Ryan wouldn't be able to match up in the long run and both he and Mike knew that.

Crawling on the dirt floor, he pushed away from Mike, knowing exactly where the handgun was. Mike's hand clamped down on the back of his leg, pulling him back. Ryan kicked at him, freeing himself for a split second before Mike clutched down on his calf muscle again. Continuing to kick, Ryan fought, gritting his teeth as he tried his hardest to get to the table where the gun was.

"You son of a bitch!"

Mike yelled, getting a hard enough grasp on Ryan that he

pulled him back again, sliding on the dirt floor. There was nothing to grab onto to stop Mike. Reaching for the table leg, it was too far away, and Ryan found himself on his back, lying face up, looking toward the ceiling. Mike stood over him, pacing in a circle as if Ryan was the lowest on the food chain and about to be sacrificed.

Mike pulled the gun from the table – the gun that Ryan almost got his hands on. If only he had moved a little faster, the whole situation would be playing out differently than it was at that moment. Mike clicked the hammer back but didn't wave it at Ryan. He aimed it about a foot away from Ryan's head, his smile full of evil as he glared down at him.

"Why'd you have to go and complicate this? Why couldn't you just let me tie you up?"

Ryan didn't answer – it was a rhetorical question and even if Mike wanted him to say something, he didn't have a response for him. He felt his heartbeat hard in his chest, so loud that Mike could probably hear it, so strong that it was palpitating through the layers of clothes he was wearing.

"I guess I'm going to have to complicate things too," Mike said, continuing to pace as he held the gun, his arm shaking. He was unsteady and even if he didn't want to shoot Ryan, his nervous tick could do him in.

Lifting his head off the floor, Ryan tried not to make any sudden movements. Mike was already on edge. He had tried to get free. He had tried to get the gun. It didn't work and now his captor was even more pissed off, willing to do anything to Ryan if he didn't play it cool.

"Why are you doing this?" Ryan asked. He had nothing to lose.

Mike knelt beside him and grabbed the rope, resuming where they had left off before Ryan's attempts to escape. He could try to attack again – Mike surely wouldn't expect him to attempt it again so soon. But Mike hadn't killed him yet. If he tried and failed again, Ryan might not be so lucky. Maybe Mike would lead him to whatever he was involved in. If he truly wanted him dead, it would have happened already.

Mike tightened the rope on his other wrist, securing his hands together. Even if Ryan tried, there was no escaping it. He followed the same pattern on Ryan's ankles, making just enough slack in the rope for him to be able to walk. If he tried to run, he'd fall flat on his face and wouldn't get very far.

"Why are you doing this, Mike?" Ryan asked again, hoping the sympathy card might help save his life.

"I want you to see, Ryan. I want you to know what's going on before I kill you. Now get up. We have a lot of ground to cover in little time. Don't you dare try to get away again. Next time I will kill you, you hear me? Your life isn't an important factor in the grand scheme of what this world has become."

Ryan stared up at Mike Rayburn – former fire chief for Harper Springs, now a man appearing to be at his wit's end, acting out in desperation over something Ryan was clueless about. Maybe between now and when they got to where they were going, Ryan could devise a plan to get away and stop whatever it was that Mike was involved with.

Ryan had no choice but to do what he was told. It meant staying alive one more day – he had come too far to die at the hands of a man he once trusted. Sooner or later, Mike would make a mistake. Until then, Ryan had to play along – for the future of his family and the future of the planet.

CHAPTER SEVENTEEN

When Steve arrived back at the shelter, Darryl and a few of the guys from the fire department were willing to help him get the deer to the storage cellar. It was cool enough down inside to keep it preserved, the cellar serving as a refrigerator. Getting it down the stairs was a challenge with Steve and Darryl walking backward, carrying the front end of the buck and the other two men at the tail end, taking each step slowly. With four men it wasn't quite as heavy, but the dead weight made it seem even heavier than it was.

Setting it in the closest corner, Steve grabbed a sheet and draped it over the deer, relieved he had made it back with the kill and also unharmed by whoever it was that had been watching him. It didn't mean they were out of harm's way – it just meant that things were fine for the time being.

"Damn, Steve, where'd you hunt this one down?" Darryl asked, patting the back thigh of the buck.

"Just north of town by the river. I was expecting to just get a jackrabbit or something and there he was."

"He should be fine down here tonight. It's cool enough in here and tomorrow we can clean it. If we keep it preserved, it'll feed us for a long time." Darryl's smile was wide, and it made

Steve feel like he had done something for Harper Springs instead of sitting around, eating up all the food, wasting space.

The other two men had already gone back to the shelter, leaving Steve and Darryl alone. It was a good moment, but unfortunately, one that would quickly be drained of joy, but Steve had to tell them. It would compromise everyone's security if he kept it all to himself.

"Sadly, the buck isn't the only thing I ran across up there." Steve looked down at the buck and back to Darryl, the older man's face full of questions without him saying a word. Continuing, Steve took a few steps back and paced in the small, cramped space. "Someone was watching me."

"What do you mean, someone?"

"I don't know. I was busy dragging the deer through the snow and when I looked up, someone was peaking from behind a tree. They ducked away quickly but looked again. The second time, they had no problem being spotted. We held eye contact and everything."

"Man or woman?"

"A man," Steve answered. "He was probably late thirties, early forties. But that doesn't matter. He's obviously a scout and now they know we have this big kill. They have reason to attack."

Darryl clicked his tongue and raked his hand through his hair, his brow creased as the words hit him. "We don't know if he was with the looters. What makes you think that?"

"They've been watching us since that first attack. They know we are working to rebuild. Do you think they'd take their eyes off us? They are going to attack. They're just waiting for the perfect time to do it." It was the first time Steve had a hard time keeping a positive attitude. "Has Ryan made it back yet?" When he got back to the shelter, they were quick to whisk the deer off to storage and he didn't have a chance to check.

Darryl shook his head, his eyes downcast. "No. He's not back yet."

"Wasn't he supposed to be back today? Didn't he say it'd only take a day to go out and scrounge up supplies?"

"That's what he said but as you know, things aren't exactly going as planned. He's gonna want to know about the person watching you hunt. You're right, whoever it was is probably with the looters and they'll be ready and willing to pounce on us knowing that we have this deer. Sadly, we've resorted to this – it probably only weights, what? A hundred or so pounds? Before this, that would've been a good kill but nothing to make anyone go crazy."

Steve rubbed his hands together, his fingers numb from all of the time exposed to the cold. He was ready to get to his cot and get some shut-eye, but his adrenaline was still pumping and he likely wouldn't get a bit of sleep.

"Maybe Ryan will make it back tonight. He's always got some kind of plan," Steve said. "We're low on so much stuff, I don't even think we could outlast the looters if it came down to a gun battle."

"Yeah, and we don't even know if they'll outnumber us. They've been making sure that we haven't gotten a good idea of the dynamic of their group. I think for now, someone needs to keep watch. It's bitterly cold out so we can come down into the storage room for a bit to thaw and go back up. This is what we'll need to watch the most. They're more interested in taking our supplies than anything else."

"I agree, Darryl." Steve didn't like the thought of having to keep watch alone in the dark – especially now that the temperature was falling well below zero degrees at night. And what if blizzard conditions started back up again? At least whoever it was that got stuck in them would have an ample amount of food and tools if they had to stick it out alone for a few days.

"Good. You take the first watch and I'll go let everyone else know." Darryl patted him on the shoulder, the corner of his mouth turning up in a small grin. "Good job, today. You're allowing us a few more weeks of good food with the kill you made tonight."

"Or a major battle – if I hadn't killed the deer, they might not be so interested in us."

Darryl laughed and shook his head. "Nah, Steve, that's not true. They've been interested in us from the moment they knew we were rebuilding Harper Springs. Deer or no deer, an attack is inevitable. The deer is just pulling us out of this mode of complacency we've been in. Time to wake back up and guard what is ours."

"See you in a few hours, Darryl." What Ryan's father said was true – the looters were after resources that would benefit them the most. Considering how sparse and ransacked the area already was, Harper Springs was like a gold mine.

❄

RYAN STOOD beside Mike Rayburn's horse, tied up like livestock at a rodeo. Mike hadn't said a word since bringing him up to ground level and though the silence might be a good thing, Ryan had a million questions he wanted answers to. Would it even matter now? Mike wouldn't let him live after all of this, so his only chance of survival was figuring out a way to escape. If he had a chance to work at it, he might be able to wiggle out of the restraints, but Mike knew what he was doing – the rope wouldn't budge, and any time Ryan moved just an inch, it dug deeper into his skin, rubbing a raw and sore spot on his wrists and ankles.

"I can hear your thinking, Ryan." Mike finally broke the silence, glancing at him from the corner of his eye.

"What am I thinking, Mike?" Maybe if he could keep the conversation going, Mike might reveal something that would be useful.

"You're trying to think of a way to untie yourself. I wouldn't bother. You know I did rodeo way back when. Steer wrestling, calf roping – I can tie a knot better than most. Doing it to you is no exception. And besides, if you run, I'll have to kill you, and I'm not ready to do that yet."

"You don't have to kill me at all, Mike."

"After seeing what you're about to do, you won't want to live. The weather is taking care of killing us off anyway."

"All because of something you're doing?" Ryan asked, prodding for more clues. He had to be careful – one wrong question and Mike might do something that Ryan couldn't come back from. He couldn't afford to get injured again. His leg was finally getting back to normal – it would be his luck that something else would happen to him.

"You're sneaky, aren't you, Ryan? All this time we worked together at the fire station, and I never realized it. A silent killer." Mike wagged his finger toward Ryan, securing a saddlebag on the horse. "Where is your horse? I presume you rode here on one, right?"

Ryan disregarded the question and continued. Maybe he could get him right where he wanted him. "What is the Atmospheric Frequency Control Project?"

The question stopped Mike in mid-step, his grin fading into a frown instantaneously. "Where's your horse, Ryan?"

"What is it?" Ryan tried to step forward, but it was more like a hop, and he almost lost his balance in the snow.

"Fine. If you don't want to answer me, you can just walk behind my horse. Seeing as you're pretty much incapacitated, that might be a hard task for you."

Damn it, he wasn't budging. Ryan motioned with his head in the direction he had left the horse. It was dark out and it took a second for Mike to spot his horse. Guiding Ryan and his horse toward it, he secured the horses together, making it where they both could walk, but if Ryan tried to get away, he'd pull Mike with him. He untied Ryan's legs so he could straddle the saddle, but kept his hands tied.

"It'll be like pack horses. I'll be the lead. And I mean it,

Ryan. Don't try to escape. Besides, why would you want to? I'm about to expose you to a world that will explain every question you have on your mind. If it wasn't for all this snow and me being pressed for time, I'd make your ass walk next to the horse."

"That's not what I'm' worried about," Ryan replied, shaking his head.

"What are you worried about, then?"

"What your plans are with me after you show me what you've been up to. It's like the saying goes – you'll tell me but then you'll have to kill me."

"You're accurate to an extent." Mike looked around, checking the cellar door and his saddlebags. "I think we have enough food and supplies to get us through to our destination. Once we're there, none of that will matter."

"Why won't it matter?"

"How about you put a stop to the questions right now? How about we ride in silence and enjoy the moon reflecting off the snow? You never were much of a talker and now suddenly, I can't get your ass to shut up."

Mike dug the heel of his boot into his horse, bringing him to life. Ryan's horse responded to the pull on the rope, following in stride with the other. It was a shame Mike had stripped him of everything – if he had his knife, he could easily cut the lead rope and make a run for it. Even if that was a possibility, Mike was armed like a one-man army and the chances of Ryan getting away before he was shot were slim to none. His curiosity was running wild – he wanted to see what Mike had been up to. In the time it took them to travel to wherever they were going, Ryan could try to devise a way to either kill Mike if necessary or get away and make it back to Harper Springs with the information he'd gathered from his trip with his former chief.

Patience wasn't his strong suit and he hated being held hostage. Mike had a gun in a holster on his hip and he was a quick draw. Ryan felt helpless, and though he was trying to play Mike for information, it was still hard to be thrown into the situation he was in. He was used to taking control and now he was having to take orders from a man that was up to no good. Ryan wasn't sure if he'd make it, but he told himself he had to. He had no idea what they were about to stumble on but by the way Mike had been acting, along with the warnings Doug spouted off before his suicide, was enough intel that could save everyone's lives.

Mike guided him toward the foothills that were at the base of the mountains. More snow fell and the temperatures were easily following well below the freezing mark. The horse hooves clomped on the snow that was now getting packed enough that they only sank a few inches into it. If more snow fell on top of it, it would soften again, but for now, the horses were gaining enough traction to keep a steady pace, which also meant they wouldn't exhaust as easily. With no vantage point or idea of how far they'd be going, Ryan wasn't sure how fast they needed to go or how long they'd be traveling.

"How far are we going?" Ryan asked though he knew that Mike wasn't in the mood to answer many questions.

Glancing over his shoulder at him, Mike grunted and pointed. "We're not going far tonight. It's too cold and I need to see what the weather is going to do in the morning. We've gotta cross over the mountains. That's our first huge step in my plan."

"You think these horses can make it?"

"Why wouldn't they be able to? I've ridden my horses through this mountain range many times."

"They aren't completely rested. It takes a fully rested horse to be able to make it up those trails. If you're thinking we're just gonna hop on over, you're mistaken. And you gotta think about the weather. These horses aren't used to snow and temperatures this cold."

Mike halted his horse and turned to face Ryan, his scowl so angry that it made Ryan think that he was about to shoot him dead right where they were.

"We are stopping at a camp I made. They'll rest tonight and then we'll get moving in the morning. It's about half a mile from here. We'll have to make do with what we have. And I can't listen to you. You'll just shoot down all my plans if it means your survival."

Mike nudged the horse again, bringing them to life. To his surprise, his horse was responding right in tune to the other, which meant it had been well trained and would probably handle the mountains fine – but with the snow and cold temperatures, nothing would work as well as it would under normal circumstances. Crossing the mountains was going to be treacherous and probably worse than outrunning tornadoes and dealing with droughts.

Ryan spotted the camp that Mike had mentioned. From the fire pit to the cleared-out spot in a nook of a hill, he could tell that this was a place that Mike often went to. How it had been left untouched was nothing short of a miracle, but it was also well hidden and out of the wind.

Mike slid off the side of his horse, helping Ryan down as well. His wrists were still tied which complicated his ability to do much of anything. As soon as his boots hit the snow below, Mike tied them back up, making Ryan hobble to the cleared area where they'd stay for the rest of the night. Falling backward, Ryan hit the ground with a hard thud.

Mike threw him a blanket and a metal camping mug, turning to the fire pit where he easily got a fire started. The flames grew and the warmth was invigorating, lighting up the sides of the hills in the middle of the darkness. The horses were close enough to keep safe and warm, which was crucial for them to perform well tomorrow.

Mike poured Ryan a cup of coffee and he guided it to his mouth, taking a sip. With his hands tied, even the simple task of drinking coffee was hard to manage but his captor showed no signs of freeing him. There was no convincing him that he wasn't going to run. If the situation was reversed, Ryan wouldn't trust him either.

Neither man spoke as they sipped the coffee, staring into the orange flames that were growing. Somehow Mike had managed to keep firewood dry – maybe he was a better survivalist than Ryan had given him credit for.

Mike scooted across the snow, reaching for a chain in the left saddlebag on his horse. He twirled a padlock on his index finger and approached Ryan, pulling a pair of handcuffs from his back pocket, his smile looking even more evil with the fire lighting up his face.

"Hold your hands out," Mike demanded, opening one of the cuffs.

Ryan complied – there was no sense in fighting any of it. It was clear that death wasn't an imminent threat yet. When his life was in danger, he'd try and make another move.

The cuffs clamped down on his skin, cold on his wrists. Mike left the rope tied together as well, adding an extra layer of security. Securing the chain, he strung it toward a tree that was about five feet away from where Ryan was sitting, wrapping it around the trunk and locking it with the padlock he had been twirling.

"I know how sneaky you are, Ryan. I can't risk you making a run for it when I fall asleep. I'd stay awake if I could but we both know we need to rest."

"If you want me to beg you to not do this, you're mistaken," Ryan spoke through clenched teeth. He wasn't in the most comfortable position on the ground and the rope dug deeper into his skin, feeling as if it was about to rub right through to his bone.

"Good. That'll save us both some time and energy."

Mike leaned back against the tree that Ryan was secured to, pulling a blanket up around him. His blanket was covering him up to just above his waist, not warming him much. The cold air nipped at him – there wasn't a chance in hell he'd get any sleep with how uncomfortable he was.

"We'll leave first thing in the morning. Until then, sweet dreams," Mike said, keeping his eyes closed as he talked.

If there was a way to get loose, Ryan would try – not to get away, but to maneuver into a more comfortable position. Judging by the moon, it was a little after midnight. With the way the night was playing out, it was going to be a long one.

CHAPTER EIGHTEEN

Steve and Darryl worked all day the next day on getting the deer cleaned and stored. They skinned the hide, hoping someone might know how to make use of it for some type of winter clothing or bedding. Steve wished there was a way to save the head as a trophy but without the needed supplies, no one would be able to preserve it. He'd at least cut the antlers off – not only were they decoration, but they could make knives or tools out of them.

With the storage cellar being so cool, concerns of the meat rotting weren't at the forefront of anyone's mind. If it got any colder outside, everything inside would be on the brink of freezing. Steve slipped the meat into the hole in the wall next to the boar meat that they'd need to cook off soon – it had been a few days and though it was all-natural, he feared that even though it was staying cool, it would eventually go bad. They could always keep it out on the snow – there was plenty of ice to get the job done, but someone would have to stand guard and protect it from animals and looters.

Wiping his hands down the front of his clothes, he was surprised at how much blood was on them. Laughing, he set the knife down next to Darryl and stood up, taking some tension off of his back.

"What's so funny?" Darryl asked, looking up at him, filleting a few more pieces away from the bone.

"Nothing. We just look like we've been in here chopping up a human being or something."

"I wouldn't joke about that," Darryl replied with a shake of his head. "You ever hear about that soccer team up in the mountains? They got hungry enough to..."

Steve cut him off. "Yeah, yeah, I think everyone has heard about that. You think we'll ever run out of food and get hungry enough to get that desperate?"

Darryl followed him, looking down at his clothes. "I hope not. The thought of being a cannibal makes my skin crawl. But you never know. If it came down to surviving or dying, there's no telling what people will do."

"If we stay on top of the vegetables and the hunting, I think we'll be okay. Not to mention the rivers and lakes will fill up again with all the snow we're getting. There should be a good supply of fish out in them."

"We won't let it get bad. We're all too damn stubborn. I already feel like things are on their way up. If the weather would stop being so extreme, it would be even better."

Steve stared down at the mutilated carcass of the buck he had shot. They could use the bones for something too. Trying to channel the Native Americans, he remembered reading about how they used every bit of the animal and left nothing to waste. He wasn't sure how lucky they'd be to hunt down an animal of that size, so every bit meant something to them.

"I wonder where Ryan is and when he'll be back," Steve pondered. If there was anyone who wouldn't let Harper Springs completely die, it was him, but it had already been twenty-four hours since he had set off on gathering supplies and he still hadn't made it back.

"Any time now. He should've already been back."

"I wonder if anyone should go look for him."

Darryl wiped his hands on a towel and knelt on the floor, scanning the bones for any more meat. Steve didn't know him well but had learned from their time spent together that he wasn't a man of many words. His slumped body language suggested that he was worried about his son, but he wouldn't ever admit it out loud. He was a proud man and speaking how he felt showed weakness. Steve's father was a lot like him. He knew the prideful standpoint all too well.

"If anyone knows the area, it's Ryan." Darryl looked up at Steve and back down to the animal, gathering the remnants of the corpse.

"Even in weather like this? Y'all have said so yourself. Y'all have never seen snow like what has fallen here."

"I have faith in Ryan." Darryl's brow creased and his eyes scanned the storage room, surveying everything they had stockpiled.

"I do too. It's the other things out there that I worry about." Steve backed up toward the steps. They were finished butchering the deer and his focus was now on Ryan. "I think someone should look for him. What if he fell and got hurt?"

"I think we should give it more time. Let's cook off the rest of the boar meat tonight, have a nice sit-down meal with everyone, and then we can make decisions in the morning. Ryan said he'd only be gone for the day. But Ryan was never good at the concept of time before all of this happened. Without a watch or a cell phone, that skill of his is worse."

"Okay, Darryl. You know him better than me. I'll go with your plan."

"We can't go off knee-jerk reactions, Steve. I get it – he's your friend and he's my son. But everything we do now takes a small shred of thought. We run off now to go find him, we leave Harper Springs exposed. There are other men here to help protect it, but we need a definitive plan. What if we get lost or hurt out there too? I hate that I'm thinking this right now, but we can't risk the lives of everyone because of one man. The fact that it's my son out there makes it even worse, but times are different now. It's about surviving. It's about protecting what is ours."

"So, you're good with just abandoning Ryan?" Steve understood Darryl's point of view but still couldn't accept it. Maybe his and Ryan's relationship was a lot rockier than Steve had realized.

"No, I'm not saying abandon him. Just think it through before you run off too. What if it's a trap? What if that's what the looters want us to do? Fewer men here means a much easier attack for them. If Ryan isn't back by tomorrow morning, we can go looking for him. Until then, stick to the course."

Steve wasn't sure if he agreed with the older man or not. He was right – they shouldn't panic because they could fall right into something that would get them into trouble. But the thought of Ryan out there, possibly hurt or dead made his stomach hurt. Rather than continue to butt heads with Darryl, Steve went up the stairs to ground level. A fresh layer of snow had fallen since they had been working on the deer and his boots sunk into it about six inches, making his walk a bit harder.

He wasn't quite ready to go back to the shelter yet. It was about mid-afternoon, and they'd soon need to get the fire going to cook the rest of the boar meat. If the weather allowed, they'd avoid firing up a camp stove so they wouldn't have to burn off any propane. A steady snowfall drifted down from the dark clouds swirling overhead. It was tranquil and beautiful, but also a possible nuisance if it got any heavier or colder.

Walking back to the area where he shot the deer, he knew that curiosity might do him in. He wondered if he'd see the same person who was watching him, but the chances of that were slim. Who would be out there in the same spot when nothing else was going on? The whole situation had weird written all over it and when he thought about the look on the person's face, it made the hair on the back of his neck stand up.

There was a small pink stain where he had shot the deer. It was quickly fading away from the layer of snow that had fallen on top of it, but Steve could see remnants of the deed. A person who didn't know it had happened might not notice it – it was faint enough that it wasn't obvious.

Steve knelt beside it, his knee pushing down into the cold snow. He felt the wetness soak through his jeans – he'd kill for some winter clothing where he could stay outside and not shiver down to his bones. Until they killed more animals or were able to travel farther, wearing layers was about as good as it was going to get.

Taking a moment to let it all in, he looked around at everything covered in white. The tree branches, the ground, the hills, and the distant mountains. For a second, it felt like he was stuck in a Christmas card or a quaint village far away from the hustle of real life. The crackling in the snow pulled him from his fantasy and he turned to look behind him, not seeing anyone.

The hair on his neck stood up again, and he moved to a standing position, ready for anything. He had a gun on him and toyed with the idea of having to pull it out and use it on something other than an animal.

Hearing the footsteps again, Steve tried to gauge where they might be coming from. Turning on his heel, he did a complete three-sixty circle to look around him. And then he saw the same person, peering from around a tree, leery to come out, especially when they made eye contact again. Steve held his hand out, motioning that he had no intention of harming them... unless they made a move at him as well.

"Who are you?" He tried not to raise his voice but spoke loudly so the person could hear him. "Do you need something?"

The man took it as an invitation to completely reveal himself. Steve didn't recognize him, and the man was dressed like he was prepared for the winter weather – his boots were in good shape, his jeans were covered with leather chaps, and he had a large bag that looked to be full of things to keep him alive for a long time. Judging by his long beard, he had been out in the balance for a while.

"You live in Harper Springs?" The stranger's voice was deep and gruff, not matching his young face under all the facial hair.

"Who wants to know?"

"No need to be hostile, mister. I'm just asking a question."

Steve felt a pang of guilt and forced a smile, still trying to keep his defenses up until he could figure out what this man's intentions were.

"I don't take kindly to giving out information to looters." It was an assumption, but Steve couldn't risk it.

"Looters? Who says I'm with looters?" Though the man looked young, he seemed wise. He wasn't willing to give away too much information, just like Steve. It was another reason he couldn't trust him – he couldn't allow himself to be manipulated.

"What exactly do you want?" Steve took a step forward, the weight of the gun in his pocket a reminder that he might have to use it and do something he never had before – kill or injure a man.

"I've been wandering around this area for a few days now. Came down from Kansas. I know that you have no reason to believe me, and I understand your hesitation in giving me any information."

"Kansas, huh? How's it look over that way?" Steve asked.

"Not much different than this. Everything is leveled. Hardly anyone made it. Those who did are starving and dying of infections. I can't believe it." He shook his head and clicked his tongue as he looked down at the ground.

"What made you come to Texas?"

"To see if we could find something better. My family is all gone. They didn't make it. All resources up there are wasted. But as I've traveled, I can only see that nothing is getting better. And I also saw something you might want to know. Just yesterday."

Steve arched his eyebrow, reminding himself to take everything with a grain of salt. Everyone was losing their minds – it would've been easy for a man up to no good to concoct a story like this.

"What's that?"

"Well, first, are you a resident of Harper Springs?"

"I am." Steve nodded.

"I thought you might know that I saw a man that rode out of your town on horseback get taken at gunpoint."

Steve's heart skipped a beat, his eyes widened, and if he wanted to pretend the stranger's story didn't interest him, he was failing miserably.

"What'd he look like?"

"Tall, dark hair, about your age. The man who took him was a little older, mustache, heavier set."

It wasn't a thorough description but enough for Steve to figure that it was probably Ryan – and the description of his captor sounded a lot like Chief Rayburn. But why would he take Ryan hostage? That didn't make any sense.

"Did you see which way they went?"

"West, toward the mountains. I couldn't track for long, as I don't have a horse and they were going pretty fast, considering the weather conditions."

"How'd you know our town is called Harper Springs?" Steve was still hesitant, and it wasn't like there were highway signs or mileage markers letting people know where they were.

"I've been through here before. I was a truck driver before the shit hit the fan. I'm somewhat familiar with the area and that's why I decided to head this way. Figured the farther south I went, the more the frigid winter would let up, but I was mistaken."

Steve reached out to shake his hand. It was plausible enough that he couldn't doubt it and he had his worries about why Ryan hadn't made it back yet. "I appreciate the information. You're welcome to come back to town with me if you'd like." He omitted the news about killing the buck – he still didn't want to give too much information out. Even if the stranger wasn't part of the big looter group, desperation made people do crazy things.

"I don't think I'll dip into your supply. I'm headed further south." The man tipped his hat to Steve and returned the handshake. "Be careful out there. And if that is someone you know who got taken, I hope it all works out."

Steve went to say something else, but the man walked past him, not giving him a chance to say anything. It was almost like a dream or a figment of his imagination. It took him a few seconds to snap out of it but his flight-or-fight response kicked in and he had to get back to town and let Darryl know what he had heard. Darryl's nonchalant attitude about Ryan not making it back bothered him – maybe this would light a fire under him and kick him into gear about finding out exactly what had happened to Ryan.

CHAPTER NINETEEN

"What do you mean, someone took him?" Cecilia felt her heart race, impatient to wait for Steve to continue. He had come back to the shelter flustered, the first words out of his mouth informing them that Ryan was possibly kidnapped.

"Exactly what I mean, Cecilia. I went back to the spot where I shot the deer, and this guy was there. He said he saw someone take Ryan at gunpoint."

"Where? What direction?" She was trying hard not to lose her cool, but her husband was in immediate danger and they were standing around.

"Calm down, Cecilia. How do we know what Steve was told is credible?" Darryl stepped forward, putting his hand on her arm. She fought the urge to jerk it away from him, gritting her teeth at her father-in-law.

"Does that even matter? The longer we stand around here the worse off he could be or the farther they will get away."

"The guy described the captor like Chief Rayburn," Steve replied with a shrug.

"That right there tells me whoever told you this information is full of shit." Darryl threw his hand in the air and walked away, circling as he paced. "Chief Rayburn and Ryan worked together. Why would he take him hostage? That doesn't make any sense!"

"That's what I thought." Steve agreed, his lips pursed as he tried to figure it all out.

Ryan's recent conversation with Cecilia crept up in her memory and though he didn't want too many to know about it, now was the time to let everyone know about his suspicions. Too much was happening now to be coincidental and if it meant his safety, she didn't care if the whole world knew about his assumptions.

"There's more to this than y'all know." Cecilia steadied her voice, making sure Ty was out of earshot. He wasn't stupid – just from how they were acting, he knew something was going on, but keeping the details to a minimum might help him not realize how much danger his father was actually in.

"What is going on?" Steve genuinely seemed concerned, much more than Darryl, which made Cecilia even angrier.

Taking a deep breath, Cecilia tried to think of a way to explain it without it taking too much time. She didn't know who the mysterious stranger was who had informed Steve that Ryan was taken but considering the back story, it was plausible to her.

"Ryan has suspected that Chief Rayburn might be up to something. When he left yesterday to gather supplies, he was going to see what he could find out."

"What could Chief possibly be up to?" Darryl asked, his tone sarcastic as if Ryan had lost his mind.

"That's what he was trying to go figure out. His main suspicion was that he was working with the looters. He wanted to make sure we were protected and that he wasn't giving them information that could help them attack us."

"So, if that's true and Chief Rayburn is the one who took him, where do we need to start looking?" Steve showed interest which was refreshing compared to how Darryl was acting. Cecilia had to fight her anger, desperately attempting to not blow up at her father-in-law.

"Where are the looters staying? Where is their main area?" Cecilia inquired, looking to both men for answers.

"They're drifters, I think. Mindy might know." Steve motioned toward Mindy who was across the room. Joining them, Steve kept his voice low, asking, "Did the looter group have a home base that they would meet at?"

"Not when they had me. We were over in New Mexico and base camp was usually wherever we stopped for the night. We never stayed in one place for more than twenty-four hours."

"Well, we know their focus has been on Harper Springs. Maybe they won't be too far away."

Cecilia felt the heat rise to her face, the anger coursing through her. "I don't think we can go on maybes. He came through for us. We have to do something about this." Her hands shook and she raked them through her hair to try and calm herself down. No matter what she did, she couldn't get herself to come down the emotional roller coaster long enough to think up a rational thought.

"Cecilia... I..." Darryl began to speak, but she cut him off almost instantly.

"He's your son, Darryl. And I'm telling you right now, he suspected that Chief Rayburn was up to something. And you know better than anyone that when Ryan senses something, you can rely on it. Now, what he thinks he might be up to, I wish I could tell you. That is what he was trying to figure out." Cecilia scoffed and checked on Ty. Thank goodness he seemed oblivious to everything. "I mean, Ryan couldn't even call him Chief anymore. That seems pretty intense."

Steve patted her on the arm. "I believe it. If Ryan thought he was up to something, chances are, he probably was. And we can sit and speculate the why all day but that still won't get us closer to finding him."

"So, what do we do?" Darryl asked, his demeanor changing completely from reluctant, to ready to set out to help find Ryan.

"We go out and look for him. The last place the guy saw him

was at Rayburn's ranch. How far could they have gotten in all this snow? We should probably get a move on and head that way. Tracking them won't be hard since there will be footprints and hoof prints everywhere." Steve motioned toward Mindy, pulling her in for a side hug. "I'll let everyone know. Some of the guys from the firehouse will probably want to go but we need some of them to stay here in case this is a trap. They know Ryan is important to a lot of people here – if we all set off to look for him, they might do a sneak attack when there aren't enough of us here to defend Harper Springs."

"Good thinking, Steve." Darryl pulled a gun from under the pillow on his cot. "I'll go with you. You don't need to be out there by yourself in case they get you too."

A step in the right direction made Cecilia calm down some but she wouldn't fully relax until she saw Ryan back in the shelter, safe and sound. Until then, she'd have to put on a brave front for Ty. It was going to be the hardest thing she ever had to do.

❄

RYAN HADN'T SLEPT a wink all night. Mike had no problem, and he was left watching his captor enjoy sleeping bliss. Even if he wasn't tied up, the cold temperatures were unbearable, and he wondered how Mike was able to. With a fire going, it made it a little more comfortable, but the flames had died down, the embers flickering a bright orange against the night sky.

Shifting his weight, he felt the ropes dig into his skin. The cold metal of the handcuffs was frigid against his raw wrists, and he immediately regretted trying to move. Mike had secured him well and there was no way he'd get free – he'd have to be a contortionist to have a fighting chance.

The chain clanked when he tried to get back into his original position, causing Mike to stir from the echo. It wasn't a loud sound but in the dense air, the sound traveled well, heightening the sense of sound. His eyebrows raised and he opened his eyes for a split second, not registering what was going on around him before he drifted back to sleep.

Ryan's body shivered and even if there were blankets available, there was no staying comfortable. Sleet began to fall, bouncing off his jeans before hitting the ground next to him. It was a nice form of entertainment, but the precipitation got heavier, transitioning to freezing rain. If he stayed where he was for too long, he'd die from hypothermia. His toes and fingers were beginning to feel numb, and frostbite would set in within a matter of a few minutes if the situation didn't change.

Rather than try and keep Mike asleep, he began to move more, making the chains rattle. Kicking his feet out, he sloshed the snow underneath, attempting to make as much noise as possible to get him to wake up.

How in the hell was he sleeping through this? Ice was accumulating on them and there was no way what was left of the fire was keeping Mike warm. Ryan's movements weren't enough to wake him, so he yelled out, willing to accept the consequences. If he didn't wake him up, he'd die. If he woke him up and pissed him off, at least it'd be a quicker death.

"Mike!"

The wind began to howl, and Ryan yelled louder.

"Mike! Wake up!"

Mike lifted his head, his eyes widening when he finally realized what was transpiring around them. Sitting up, he wiped the wet from his water-resistant slicker that Ryan envied.

"Well, hell, looks like we have us a situation."

Ambling toward his horse, he pulled out a matching slicker and tossed it to Ryan, hitting him in the chest. Due to the restraints, there was no chance he'd be able to put it on, so he stared up at Mike, waiting for the next move. His body was shivering so badly that his muscles were tense, making it feel like he had just endured an hour-long workout.

"I guess you need me to untie you so you can get that on."

Mike laughed and took his time. Ryan feared frostbite was

already setting in, so he continuously moved his toes in his boots and his hands, keeping the blood flow moving just in case. His teeth chattered and Mike looked at him, his grin so snide that Ryan wished he could deck him. This wasn't a joking matter and if he moved any slower, his hostage would become a dead man.

"What's... so funny?" Ryan asked, his words coming out in short pants as his body temperature fluctuated like a person who had fallen into a frozen lake.

"Your lips are blue."

"You go any slower, Mike, and your kidnapping charge will be upgraded to murder."

Mike arched his eyebrow and finished the last rope, keeping Ryan's legs restrained. He aided in helping Ryan get the coat on and it was warm, but still not helping the damage that was already setting in.

"You really think we have law and order going on right now? It's every man for himself. Anarchy. You should know that. How many men have you killed through all of this? Isn't it up to four?"

Ryan's anger boiled deep within him, so strong that it seemed to thaw him out. "It's been two." Speaking through clenched teeth, he was in perfect range to reach out and strangle Mike, but it would ruin any chance of him finding out what he was up to. If he killed his source for information, there was no way of getting the issues fixed if there were any, and saving everyone.

"Really? I could swear it's more – but even with two, you've killed more than I have."

"Self-defense, and we don't have time to argue this right now." Ryan looked up at the sky. The freezing rain had now transitioned into heavy snow. "If we don't get moving, we'll lose the horses too." Where would they go? They weren't close to Mike's cellar anymore and were right at the foot of the mountains.

As if Mike could read Ryan's mind, he pointed up the side of the mountain. "I have a cave set up about a quarter mile up. It'll at least get us out of the heavy snowfall."

"And the horses? Can they make it up there with all the powder on the ground?"

"There's a thin layer of ice underneath. They can get traction from that. But there isn't room in the cave for them. We'll have to leave them out in the weather."

"A death sentence for them. And then how will we travel? You haven't even told me how far we are going but we sure as hell won't be able to make it over these mountains on foot, especially in winter conditions. It doesn't sound like you've thought this through very well."

Mike balled his fist and reared back, punching Ryan in the face. He fell backward, tasting copper flavor and thick liquid on his tongue. Mike stood over him, his fist still ready for another blow but backed away. Neither man spoke as he helped Ryan up, freeing him from the ropes as he got him on the horse. They still tied together like pack horses and even though it was dangerous to travel that way considering the situation, Ryan wouldn't be able to convince Mike to free him. It was a prime time to escape but Mike would never believe he had no intention of fleeing – it was best to stick together, even if they were against each other and Mike was up to something that was apparently killing off all living existence from earth.

The trek up toward the apparent cave Mike had mentioned was hell. The horses were slipping and sliding in the slush, their hooves sliding over the lower layer of ice like it was a thin sheet of glass. Ryan was lucky to know how to ride – a novice rider would've easily been tossed off the horse and injured. His horse lifted his front two legs, neighing loud to toss Ryan from his back. Holding the reigns and tightening his legs around the midsection of the horse, he stayed on, slipping enough that he almost lost control. Despite his current health condition of almost freezing to death, he fought, unwilling to succumb to the harsh weather surrounding them.

Mike had troubles too, but Ryan was focused on his own. He spotted the cave about one hundred yards ahead of them and pressed on, fighting the horse's will to stop. Sliding off the side, he stayed in Mike's line of sight before the man tried to shoot him. Guiding the horses, he pointed toward an area beside the cave that was blocked by trees and the side of the mountain.

"The snow is still falling but this will be a great wind block to keep the horses out of direct contact," Ryan said as he tied them to the trunk of the nearest tree. "They'll stand a fighting chance right here."

The wind howled and Mike said something, but Ryan didn't even try to get him to repeat it. Following him inside the cave, he was surprised to see a fire pit ready to go, along with some wood stacked near the entrance. Mike pulled out a lantern and lit it with a match, lighting up the small shelter.

"Gather up some logs and get the fire going," Mike demanded as he balled his fists and blew into them.

Ryan did as he was told – remembering Mike had a gun and wasn't hesitant with it, now wasn't the time to make him even edgier. Piling up a few logs, he poured a few drops of propane on the wood to get it to ignite and tossed a match into it. The flames were large for a few seconds before burning the fuel off, the warmth of the fire the best thing he had felt in a long time.

The roar of the fire along with the howling wind just outside the front of the cave made it feel like the setting of a horror movie. It was a shame this wasn't fiction, and he was living a real-life scary story playing out before his very eyes. Holding his hands up to the fire, Ryan literally felt like his flesh was thawing out like a piece of meat left out on the cabinet. He wondered if any wildlife had made a home within the cave – maybe they could hunt something down and have a good meal.

"Good thinking with the horses," Mike said, unwilling to make eye contact with Ryan.

The flames cast huge shadows on the wall of the cave behind Mike, and Ryan watched them dance around for a few seconds, admiring the show.

"I wouldn't hold your breath on them being there when we're

able to leave again. They're protected against the wind, but it is still unbearably cold out there."

"In all this bullshit, I have to try and be positive about it." Mike finally looked up from the fire, looking right into Ryan's eyes.

"I can't find a reason to be positive, Mike. You're holding me hostage, you won't tell me what the hell is going on, and you've made it clear that once I do find out what you've been up to, I'd rather die than try to keep surviving. So, you know what? I don't give a shit if the horses are there. I don't give a shit if we ever leave this cave." Some of Ryan's statement was false – he wanted to get back to Cecilia and Ty. He wanted to make sure they were okay. But Mike had completely frustrated him, and the man didn't deserve to know Ryan's true feelings about anything.

"I know I've let you down, Ryan. I never knew it'd get like this."

"What? What did you not think would get like this?" Ryan raised his voice, and it echoed off the back of the cave.

Mike looked away again, poking the fire with a stick. "Now's not the time. Soon."

It took everything Ryan had within him to keep his cool. He never was a man of patience and sadly, Mike's behavior was not helping him develop any. *Soon.* That word was relative – what was soon for one person felt like an eternity to another. With the blizzard raging on outside the cave, seconds seemed like years. Ryan wasn't sure how much more of it he could take.

CHAPTER TWENTY

Ryan wished he could sleep. His body was giving out on him, but his mind was running a mile a minute, unwilling to allow him just a few minutes of shut-eye. Mike would doze from time to time, his eyes closing, his body relaxing, only for him to jolt awake and make sure Ryan was still there. The fire was dying, and Ryan poked it with a stick, turning the small pieces of wood that remained in the pit.

"We need more wood." Ryan's tone was stern and though he didn't yell, it echoed off the cave walls.

"We don't have any." Mike was groggy and opened his eyes for a few seconds before snuggling his coat up around his midsection. Leaning back against the wall, he yawned and closed his eyes. "How about you walk over to the cave entrance and see what the weather is doing? And before you try anything stupid, remember I have a gun pointed right at you."

Ryan forced his body to move, the normal task proving to be challenging. His muscles were tight, his body ached, and it took a second for the blood to begin flowing to his extremities. It was like learning to walk all over again but once he got to a complete standing position, it felt good to get moving.

"Mike, you've been dozing for the past several hours. And

I'm not tied up. If I wanted to escape, don't you think I would've done it by now?" Ryan had to remind himself to stop with the smart-ass remarks, but he couldn't help it. His nerves were shot, and he was tired of them dragging their feet. He needed to know what was going on soon or he feared worse things would happen.

"I don't remember you having that mouth on the fire department." Mike sat up and glared at him, the gun in his hand, ready to go if need be.

Ryan ignored his remark and ambled to the entrance of the cave, peering out. He couldn't see where the horses were – the angle wasn't right to be able to check, but the sun had come out and the snow had stopped falling. It was still very frigid out and nothing was melting, but at least they would be able to see where they were going.

"It stopped snowing, Mike." Ryan moved back inside, sitting beside the embers that would soon die off. "I'd say another foot of snow has fallen out there but it's hard to tell. We are lucky it didn't cover the cave up."

"Why didn't it?" Mike asked, curiosity in his voice.

"I guess we were positioned just right on the edge of the cliff that anything that fell just didn't have a place to land and went farther down the mountain."

"And the horses?"

"Couldn't tell. I'm a little worried about what kind of traction they'll be able to get in the new snow. Nothing has been up this way to pack it down and make it hard. And if as much snow has fallen as I think, they're going to fall right down in it. So are we."

"I'll take my chances."

Ryan let Mike's last remark linger, hovering like the smoke from the fire. Both men sat in silence for a few minutes, Ryan coming up with millions of questions he'd like answers to.

"How much farther are we going?"

Mike looked up at him, his brow creased, but he still didn't answer him.

"What is this Atmospheric Frequency Control Project that I read back at your cellar?"

Mike gave him the same look as just moments before, grabbing the stick they had been using to stoke the fire. Sparks flew up and small flames shot out of the charred wood, which was a miracle because there wasn't much else to burn.

"Why are you so curious?"

Ryan shook his head and bit his bottom lip, attempting to choose his words wisely. "You're kidding, right? You hold me hostage, tell me I'd rather die than try to save everyone once I find out what you're up to, and then you ask why I'm curious?" Ryan patted his chest and clicked his tongue. "How do you expect me not to be curious?"

"We are headed just past the New Mexico border. In the badlands where the foothills are."

"That's at least another twenty miles or so," Ryan replied. "If the horses are even out there, that'll take several more days under these conditions." Mike wasn't giving much of a response to Ryan's travel concerns, so he focused on another question. It felt like he might be able to pull more information out of Mike if he kept going and didn't show his frustrations.

"What will we find when we get to the badlands?"

"You ever hear of ways to control the weather?"

"Yes. They broached the subject in the weather spotting classes I took."

Mike shifted his weight and straightened his posture, making eye contact with Ryan for the first time in about ten minutes. "And what are your thoughts on it?"

"I'm not sure, Mike. Where are you going with this? Are you telling me that you've been controlling the weather?"

"We're not far off now. You'll see when you get there."

Anger coursed through Ryan so fast that he saw red. He couldn't keep a handle on it any longer and though Mike held the gun that had been trained on him for the past day, he wasn't worried about the pull of the trigger any longer.

"No, Mike! Damn it, do you realize how many people have suffered? How many people are still suffering? Jesus, man! Tell me what the hell is going on before this gets worse than it already is. Hell, I'm not sure if it can. We're already crippled!"

Mike held his hand up, stopping Ryan. "Don't ever ask if it can get worse, because believe me, it can."

"Then why keep this going? What benefit are you getting out of it?"

"It goes farther than what you can comprehend, Ryan."

Ryan scoffed and paced, unable to sit still any longer. Despite his sleep deprivation, the rush of adrenaline from his anger had given him his second wind.

"Try me, Mike. Maybe if you'd give me more information, I'd understand it a tad bit better. We have to stop dragging our feet! People are dying, Mike! Your family! Is whatever you're up to worth everything that has happened?"

"It's too late." Mike's voice shook but he quickly masked it. "We can't reverse anything anymore. You'll see soon. Let's get out there and see if the horses are there. Then we gotta get moving."

Ryan wanted to deck him but instead, did as Mike told him. This was something huge and he was on the brink of finding out exactly what it was. Another twenty miles – hopefully, everything would hold out long enough for them to get there.

❄

STEVE'S HORSE was having a hard time fighting through the deep snow. If it wasn't for the fact that they'd completely exhaust themselves by walking, he'd suggest leaving the animals behind – they weren't traveling much faster than they were on foot, but at least they weren't getting tired from the miles they were putting in.

"We're not going to be able to go as far as usual," Darryl said, edging his horse up next to Steve's. "They've already been running them ragged and now, with the snow, they are going to need to rest a lot more often than usual."

"I was just thinking the same thing."

Steve's patience, once strong and steady, was now running completely thin. He tried to remain positive but with hurdle after hurdle jumping in front of them, he was beginning to wonder if this was all a lost cause. He'd never do as Doug had and take his own life, but what exactly were they fighting for now? A planet that had apparently betrayed itself and gone crazy? If that were true, it was all at the hands of human beings and their scientific developments that proved detrimental to the environment.

He was keeping one eye on the tracks in the snow, and one eye looking forward, making sure they weren't being trailed. They were going through uncharted waters and there was no way to know what to expect. Was it Mike that really had Ryan? Was Ryan really kidnapped or had he just not been able to make it back to Harper Springs yet? Were they completely overreacting to whatever may be occurring? There were too many what-ifs and unknowns, and it was bad enough to drive a sober man to drink, a sane man to an asylum, and a once optimistic man to the depths of negativity.

"Looks like the tracks are pretty consistent with heading northwest. And there are more than one set of them. Looks like they are on horseback." Steve observed the ground below, hoping he'd be able to find any sign that it was Ryan that they were tracking. Had he dropped something, it would've easily been buried by the heavy snowfall that pushed through the area through the nighttime hours. It was a miracle they could still see the tracks – they were faint, but the snow had left a good enough outline for them to be able to tell someone had been through. If any more snow had fallen, they'd be completely covered up, giving them an even bigger challenge.

"You know, we've been without technology for all these months since the tornadoes and I still find myself reaching into my pocket for my cell phone to call him. That's a hard habit to break but I wish I could get him on the line to check on him."

Steve clenched his jaw, remembering how just a few hours ago Darryl was hesitant to even go look for his son. He didn't have a back story on his and Ryan's relationship, nor was it his business, but just by the way Darryl had acted, it seemed to be rocky.

"Yeah, times like this make us all think about the things we took for granted. Electricity, running water, cell phones, internet..." Steve trailed off, gazing down at the sparkling snow. "What's your gut feeling telling you? Do you think Mike has him?" Maybe Steve was opening a can of worms in asking him, but it beat the silence between them and the rhythmic clomp of the horse's hooves sloshing through the snow and ice.

"If Mike has him, I want to know why. Mike was the chief of the fire department here. Ryan was a firefighter on that department. I can't bring myself to believe that he took Ryan maliciously. There is a lot more to this than we know, if it is even Mike who took him."

"I haven't seen him around town lately. If it ain't him, where has he been?"

Darryl shrugged. "Hell, if I know. I've been confused since all this bullshit started. Still, no help coming our way. It's never snowed this much here. And now it's like we're in some crazy survival movie where it's turning into every man for himself. A part of me hopes I eventually wake up in my bed and this was either one long nightmare, or I was in a coma from something else and my mind conjured up the whole damn thing."

"So that would make me a figment of your imagination." Steve laughed and focused back on the tracks. "Unfortunately, I'm not just something your dreams made up. I'm here, in the flesh, and we are riding through several feet of snow, looking for your son."

"I know. But sometimes I have to pretend it's the other or I'm going to end up doing what Doug did and blow my brains out. If it wasn't for Ryan, Cecilia, and Ty, I probably would've done it already. I'm an old-timer. I've lived a good life. I don't want to go out like this."

"You won't. Better days are bound to be in front of us."

Both men fell silent again, the horse's steps crackling through layers of snow and ice, struggling to gain traction as they sunk into the cold. Steve tried to keep track of how long they had been riding. By the position of the sun, or what little they could see of it, they had been going for a couple of hours, and by the pace of the horses, they were losing energy.

Coming up to the edge of the foothills, he slid off the saddle and led the horse to a tree, tying him up. Darryl followed suit, not asking any questions – he was probably aware of the stamina and health conditions of their only means of transportation.

Steve stretched his legs out, feeling the snow seep through his jeans. His boots held good protection and were waterproof, protecting his feet and keeping them warm. Trudging through, he continued to follow the tracks left behind. Spotting a small cove in the hills, he tried to hurry as best as he could, his legs burning as he fought the depth of the snow.

There was a small pit set up for a fire and what looked like a campsite. Due to its position against the hills, very little snow had fallen around it, just enough to dust the ground. He heard Darryl's footsteps behind him and waited, glancing over his shoulder at the older man.

"Looks like someone has been camping here. And by the looks of the fire pit, it's been recent," Steve said, circling it.

"Could it be Ryan or possibly a looter who has been watching us?"

Steve shrugged and knelt beside the pit, running his finger over a piece of charred wood that was now covered in ice. "By the number of tracks, it was probably more than one person, but past that, I wouldn't be able to tell who it was." Leaning back against the hill, he slid down to the ground, the icy cold soaking through the fabric of his pants. "What if we're not chasing the right tracks? What if this was just some drifter or someone who is part of the looters? Or even worse! They are leading us in the wrong direction!" Steve tried not to feel discouraged but there was just no way to know for sure.

"That man you talked to said they went this way, right?" Darryl remained standing, walking back and forth as he observed the campsite.

"Yeah, but I don't know him. What if he was part of the plan to get us on a wild goose chase?"

Darryl pondered Steve's question for a second, looking up at the sky and back down. "We have to try. It's better to get out here and try than it is to just sit around Harper Springs, twiddling our thumbs and hoping for the best."

"But the horses... and our clothes. Not to mention our food." Steve closed his eyes and gritted his teeth. "I need something to prove we are going in the right direction. That we should even be out here looking for him!" He raised his voice and it echoed, making some birds fly off nearby trees, their wings flapping loudly.

"We're in fine shape right now. We are taking a break to rest the horses. We still have plenty of food. I think we're going the right way. Ryan would be doing the same for us if this were reversed." Darryl sat beside Steve and patted his leg. "Don't die out on me now, Steve. I know just a few minutes ago I mentioned wanting to do what Doug did, but I need to find my son. I need to make sure he gets back to his family."

Steve tried not to say it, but he just blurted it out before he could stop himself. "Back in town, you didn't seem the least bit interested in the possibility of Ryan being kidnapped."

Darryl forced a small smile. "I know. Because I didn't figure it'd be possible that the accusations against Chief Rayburn were true. But then I came to realize that nothing is as it seems. Nothing will ever be how it was. And then the possibility became more realistic. We gotta keep going. The why's and what if's will eventually be answered if we don't give up. You have been the voice of reason, the happy-go-lucky guy since I met you. If you're going to become the dark and brooding one, we're gonna have some problems. That's mine and Ryan's job."

Steve laughed and chewed on the inside of his cheek as he thought about Darryl's words. He was right – Ryan wouldn't even hesitate to be out in this if it meant saving them. "Okay, Darryl. Let's get back to it."

CHAPTER TWENTY-ONE

To both Ryan and Mike's surprise, the horses had survived the night. Putting them in between two sides of the mountain helped serve as a shelter. They weren't in the best of shape to ride for long distances, but they would be healthy enough to carry them farther and faster than their legs would be able to. Looking over his shoulder, Ryan checked to see if anything was behind them, whether it was a wild animal to kill for food or possible looters, he had a sneaking suspicion that they weren't alone on their trip.

For a moment, he pondered if it could be someone from Harper Springs, out to look for him. Steve would probably eventually realize that he hadn't made it back, and if he hadn't paid attention, Cecilia would be making noise that his arrival back home was much later than anyone had anticipated. Making sure Mike wasn't looking, he pulled the pocketknife from his pants and carved his initials into the tree trunk where he had the horses tied. Moving quickly, he put an R and a G as best as he could, the bark so wet that it fell off just by touching it. If someone was out looking for him, hopefully, they'd catch on and see it, and if they had, know what it meant.

"You ready to get going?"

Mike's voice made Ryan jump and he took a few steps away from the tree, slipping the knife back into his pocket. Without answering him, he climbed up on his horse and waited, hoping to keep Mike's attention from the tree. Leading them away, Ryan tossed him the reins to his horse, keeping their backs turned away from the tree.

Mike tied the horses together, just like he had done the day before. They were headed to New Mexico and though it wasn't that far away, in the current conditions it could take a lot longer than usual.

It was back to silence between the two men, the cracking of the snow the only sound. Ryan watched the sky – the sun was trying to break through the clouds but with each passing second, the northern sky seemed to be getting darker and the wind picked up, chilling him to the bone.

"I think there's another cold front coming in." Ryan pointed north, fearing that another large storm might be the death of them. He already had shown early signs of hypothermia – thankfully, he had recovered nicely, but another occurrence could prove fatal for him.

"There is a gap in the mountain range just over there. We get through that and it's smooth sailing to our destination." Mike ignored the fact that regardless of where they chose to cross over to the New Mexico state line, it wouldn't stop the weather from bearing down on them.

"I don't know if we have time for that, Mike. Do you have another hiding place somewhere?"

"No. That cave was my last camp before getting to my destination."

"You've been coming this way for a while, haven't you?" Ryan asked, still in disbelief over what Mike could be up to and how he ever could've gotten involved in something so drastic.

"Since before the tornadoes started, Ryan."

"I can't..." Ryan cut himself off, shocked, hurt, and curious about the whole thing. He couldn't allow himself to be angry.

Anger would get him into even more trouble, and they were so close he could taste it. There were a few more obstacles between him and finding out the truth, the most crucial one at that moment being the cold front speeding south, coming right for them. They were pawns in Mother Nature's game again, almost as if the anomaly had something personal against Ryan.

"Looks like another blizzard," Mike replied, the emotion completely wiped from his tone.

"Step on it, Mike! We gotta get moving!" Ryan urged his horse to go faster, but since Mike's horse was on the lead rope, he was stuck. "If you want to make it through this, we gotta go. We are stuck right in the middle of whatever that cloud is going to bring!"

Mike finally kicked into action, nudging the side of his horse. Though the animals couldn't run fast in the deep snow, their instincts were kicking in, alerting them to find safety. The rope tightened so much that it almost snapped, and Ryan plead with his horse to keep going and stay up with Mike. The cold wind hit them like a wall and when he looked behind him, a wall of snow was falling down the side of the closest hill, barreling right at them.

The visibility fell to almost zero and by the tightening and loosening of the rope attached to Mike's horse, Ryan could gauge how much quicker he needed to make his horse go. The biggest fear now was slamming into a tree trunk, and he hoped that since Mike had traveled this way several times, he had a good vantage point on where to guide the horses.

The avalanche of snow was nipping at their heels. The horses neighed loudly, knowing at any second, they'd be killed. Ryan gripped the reins out of habit, holding on, though when the horses tumbled, he'd be taken down with them.

"Mike!"

He wasn't sure why he was yelling his name. The snow enveloped them, the icy cold taking Ryan's breath away as the force of the precipitation tripped the horses, sending them all toward the earth below. Ryan couldn't see what was going on and expected pain as he hit, but the soft powdery snow cushioned his fall. Holding his breath, he closed his eyes as the snow wall buried him as his body continued to slide down the side of the hill.

It felt like an eternity that he couldn't breathe. Opening his eyes, his body finally came to a standstill, and he realized he was buried under the mounds of freezing ice and snow. Moving quickly, he knew he had to get himself out. He needed oxygen and he also didn't want to freeze to death. His clothes were soaked, providing extra pounds to carry as he frantically dug through the barrier, his body screaming for him to get to the surface. It was so dark that he feared he wasn't even digging in the right direction, but as he went, the layers got thinner and easier to dig through, and when his head popped out, it was the best breath of fresh air he had ever gotten.

Ryan's first concern was Mike. Looking around, he tried to spot dark clothing in the snow. When he tried to stand, his head pounded and he felt liquid drip from his forehead, some stopping on his lip. When he licked, he tasted the metallic thickness and touched where his hairline and forehead met. There was a gash, though he couldn't tell how big.

Pulling himself to a standing position, he almost fell when he took a step. A combination of vertigo and newly fallen snow hindered his ability to walk, and he landed on his knees. Crawling might have been a better option, so he stayed on his hands and knees, searching for a man he needed to be alive, even if it was just for a bit longer so he could get him to their destination. The wall of snow had stopped once they had reached the bottom and though that was over, the howling wind made it even colder as it blew up against Ryan's wet clothes.

"Mike!" He regretted yelling – his pulse pounded in his head, making pain shoot down his neck and into his spine. He couldn't worry about a possible head or neck injury. He had to find Mike or getting as far as they had would be for nothing.

His eyes scanned again, and a jolt of energy shot through him when he saw the snow moving about twenty yards from where he was. Mike shot through the surface much as he had, gasping at the air, freeing himself from the snow grave they both had involuntarily been placed in. Ryan helped him up, shocked at the color of his skin and lips. For all he knew, he looked the same, but he didn't have a mirror, nor did he care. At least they both had survived the avalanche.

"That was a close one." Mike's teeth chattered as he spoke, his eyes widening when he finally got a look at Ryan. "Your head is bleeding." He pointed up at Ryan's forehead.

"I know. We need to find a place to warm up and dry our clothes. I lost my bag with all of my stuff in it." He patted his arms and shivered. "How much farther are we going? We lost the horses too."

"Just over there." Mike pointed again, a wide grin forming on his lips.

Ryan followed his index finger, his heart skipping a beat at the sight that Mike was pointing out. It was about half a mile away, sunk in a valley, giving them the perfect vantage point to look down at what Ryan presumed was the Atmospheric Frequency Control Project that Mike had been working on. It was like nothing Ryan had ever seen, and though he was finally getting his first glimpse of it, a million questions popped into his mind – the very first being, "How in the hell have you managed to keep the snow and ice off of it?" It was untouched by the weather and in perfect condition, like an oasis stuck right in the middle of the desert.

❄

STEVE FELT like he was getting sick. A combination of the cold air and not being appropriately dressed for their journey was making his chest hurt. When he coughed, it was dry and unproductive, feeling like a bunch of rocks was bouncing around in his lungs. Both he and Darryl wheezed, both sounding like they and bronchitis or pneumonia. If they were out much longer, that would be a reality – and pneumonia was already a serious sickness – now, it was likely deadly for anyone who got it.

The horses were struggling almost as badly as they were, but he refused to call off the search mission. His inspiration was remembering how Ryan had helped him when the looters had taken him hostage. This was the least he could do for his friend, even when it felt like he could collapse into the snow and drift off into oblivion.

"The tracks go up to that cave, it looks like," Steve said, squinting against the bright sun reflecting off the snow. "The tracks are getting harder to see. It must've snowed a lot harder up this way."

"Yeah, higher elevation means more precipitation." Darryl followed him up, both men not talking much to help conserve energy.

"There's a cave." Steve slid off his horse and tied it up, cautiously entering the dark cave. Clicking his flashlight on, spotting another fire pit that looked to have recently been used. "Well, someone was here too. I want to say it's the same people, but we really can't go off assumptions."

"Two people – there are two different types of bootprints outside."

Steve checked for supplies. The place had been stripped clean. He took a second to catch his breath and get a break from the cold wind. The inside of the cave wasn't warm in the least, but without the wind chill making the temperature plummet, it was comfortable. What he'd give for a piping hot mug of coffee, dry clothes, and a heater blasting right on his face.

"Steve! You might want to come to see this." Darryl's voice echoed at the entrance of the cave, pulling Steve from his daydream of warmth and comfort.

Hurrying outside, he turned the corner where the snow didn't seem to be quite as deep. There were horse hoof prints everywhere. Darryl was pointing at a tree and Steve's eyes followed it. Carved in the trunk were the letters R and G. It was messy and almost hard to tell what they were but clear enough to be a huge clue.

"R and G," Steve said.

"R for Ryan. G for Gibson," Darryl replied, his gloved finger tracing it.

Steve knew exactly what it meant but let the other man sort it out. "You think it was him letting someone know he was here?"

"I'd be willing to bet that's the story. Someone could debunk it and say these initials were left years ago but it's too fresh. The way the bark is, the smell of the wood – it's enough evidence for me to believe that we are following the right tracks. We are right on their heels. We just have to move faster."

Steve agreed. Though they were exhausted, cold, and almost defeated, they were so close he could taste it. Before the initials, they had no clue as to whether or not they were going the right way, following the right people, or if Ryan was still alive. Despite his physical ailments, a fire was lit underneath him, and he found energy buried deep in the recesses of his body.

Climbing on the horse, he motioned for Steve to follow. "I guess we better keep moving. It appears as if they are going fast themselves, and probably are on the other side of this range. If we go now and push through, we might be able to spot them on the other side."

It didn't take much more convincing for Darryl to follow, both men pushing themselves and their horses to the limit. When they got to the top of the hills, the tracks stopped, as if Ryan and his captor had disappeared. Steve steadied his horse, knowing if he went down the other side at the speed they had been running them, they'd skid downward, killing the horses and fatally wounding themselves along with them.

"Shit, where'd the tracks go?" Steve asked out loud, looking down the hill.

"Looks like one massive snow slide."

"An avalanche. They got caught in a damn avalanche." Steve shook his head, nausea coursing up his body. "That's the only explanation as to why the tracks stopped abruptly. It's not like they just vanished." The snow was smooth, appearing completely untouched. "Son of a bitch! I hope he survived it." Steve kept his voice low – these weren't large mountains like the ones seen in movies where massive avalanches took out everything in its path – but with the large amounts of snow and the steep incline on the west side, no matter what size of the avalanche it was, it could do a lot of damage. And if they spoke too loudly, they could cause another one to happen.

"Maybe they got down off of this before it hit." Darryl clenched the reins, his eyes staying down as both men contemplated their next step.

"I guess we head down there. We won't know if he survived unless we go check and make sure."

Steve nudged his boot in the side of the horse, which refused to move at first, aware of the dangers of the incline they were about to take. After a few more seconds of convincing the animal, they started down the mountain, cautiously taking each step out of fear of falling, as well as tripping off another avalanche that could take them out in the blink of an eye.

CHAPTER TWENTY-TWO

Ryan wanted to hurry down to the valley to find out exactly what was going on. Mike stood beside him, pulling out the same gun he had been carrying through their entire trip, and pointing it at Ryan's back.

"I wouldn't move until I tell you to," Mike said through gritted teeth, the cold steel of the barrel prodding into the small of Ryan's back.

"So now that you have me here, you're going to kill me? Why not just do it back at your farm? Why waste all this time?"

Mike nudged him forward, the metal hard against his muscles, jolting him to take a step. Complying with Mike's request, Ryan did everything he was told – Mike had already proven how nervous he was with the gun and the last thing he needed was for him to accidentally pull the trigger before Ryan had the chance to get away.

"Just walk, Ryan." Mike side-stepped the question, staying behind Ryan as they progressed toward the untouched valley.

As they got closer, the depth of snow got shallower until Ryan found his feet on dry ground. His wet clothes clung to his body but even the temperature had recovered, shooting up to around seventy degrees if Ryan had to guess. The valley was lush and green, not even showing evidence that tornadoes, drought, or blizzards had ever even come through. For a second, he had to wonder if he had been shot and this was him dying. Or maybe he was dreaming and would wake back up in the winter wasteland back at Harper Springs.

There was a cabin offset from the open land and beside that, several acres of what appeared to be antennas all arranged in rows. The metal poles shot upward toward the sky, and at the top of each pole there were shorter metal poles perpendicular, forming an X that ran parallel to the ground, resembling helicopter blades, only they didn't swivel like them. It looked like something out of a science fiction movie and Ryan stood in awe, trying to figure out exactly what these antennas did. The perimeter of the area was surrounded by a chain link fence with razor wire at the top, almost like a prison sat inside.

Mike pushed him forward, reaching in his pocket for a set of keys. Unlocking the gate, they went inside, and Ryan got an even better look. The metal poles shot up about thirty feet in the air and as they got closer, he could hear a low humming noise coming from each one of them. There had to have been over one hundred total, making him feel small in the middle of the field that surrounded them.

"What... what in the hell is this?" Ryan spread his arms, motioning toward the antennas.

"The Atmospheric Frequency Control Project. You know, the thing you've been asking about the entire way here." Mike smiled and rested against the closest pole, looking up toward the sky.

"This is what has been causing all of the drastic weather?" Ryan's eyes widened. There was so much to take in that he couldn't get his mind to slow down enough to comprehend what he was witnessing. This couldn't be real. How could anyone even come up with something like this, and what was the reason behind it?

"It is. Judging by the look on your face, you want to know

how it works, right?" Mike pushed off the pole and circled it. "Just look at those clouds right above us. Absolutely beautiful. Man-controlled science happening right before your very eyes."

"Yeah, how does it work, Mike?" Maybe the less Ryan knew, the better chance he'd have of Mike not killing him, but how could he not inquire with it right in front of him? The more he knew also gave him a better chance of stopping future occurrences and they could finally rebuild without the worry of such an apocalyptic event happening again.

"These antennas shoot energy surges up into the ionosphere. You know, the upper atmosphere that runs off electrically charged atoms."

Ryan had read some about the ionosphere, but it went beyond what they taught him in his general storm-spotting classes. He made no indication he knew what Mike was talking about because this was way over his head. There were plenty of conspiracy theories about government-controlled weather and atmosphere, but he never believed much of it. Now, right before his eyes, it was happening.

"These antennas can shoot the maximum number of ions and atoms up into the atmosphere, causing a disturbance at higher levels in the ionosphere. Certain amounts of electricity can cause floods, hurricanes, tornadoes, and now the winter weather we are dealing with. It can flip the earth's magnetic poles, which it seems that has happened now that Texas is looking a lot like the North Pole. It can make the upper atmosphere like a giant magnifying glass, frying everyone underneath it, which would explain the horrible drought and high temperatures we had as well." Mike paused and took a breath, the grin on his face making the hair on the back of Ryan's neck stand up. "Hell, it can even cause earthquakes just by the shift it causes on the planet."

"Why, Mike?" It came out in a whisper. Ryan was completely shocked that anyone would ever think to do such a thing.

"We first got the idea from the military." Mike disregarded

Ryan's question and continued as if he were a salesman trying to market his creation. "They originally honed in on the ionosphere to try and control communications during the war. We played around with it a little and realized, holy shit, we can do a lot more. There's biological warfare... why not meteorological war too? Countries wouldn't be able to fight against that. You asked earlier why there was no snow right here. This is where we manipulate the ionosphere. Then it moves on, drifting away from here, leaving this as the safest spot on earth. No snow. No drought. Not even one tornado. Just damn near perfect."

"So you decide to kill off everyone? I still don't know why you're doing it! Why?" Ryan raised his voice, yelling at Mike. His anger flared and he didn't care that the gun was still aimed in his direction.

"You realize I'm going to have to kill you, right? I can't release all this information and trust you to walk away a free man. I've worked too hard to get this built. I've worked with other men. Other governments in other countries are paying me to do this. Paying us... lots of money..." Mike trailed off, his eyes moving toward the cabin where another man was walking their way. He was older and Ryan didn't know him. "Speak of the devil, here's my partner in crime now."

"I told you not to bring anyone here." The man glared at Mike. "Who is this?"

"Ryan Gibson. He was at the fire department with me."

"So, you decide to bring him along for a field trip? Son of a bitch, we're already dealing with too much right now!"

Ryan watched as the two men argued. If they continued to go back and forth, it might have been the perfect time for him to run off, but he wouldn't be fast enough. His physical health wasn't the best after his escapade through the frozen wasteland and he was certain the older man was also armed. There was no way he would be able to outrun two guns.

"I just wanted him to see what was going on before I kill him," Mike said, glancing at Ryan from the corner of his eye.

"I don't know why you're smiling, Mike. This has gotten way out of control! We were supposed to figure out a way to control the electricity sent up into the sky. We were supposed to be able to turn it off and on! And now look at us! We've practically wiped out the entire human population! This was supposed to be used for war against other countries, not against our own people!"

"We're getting there," Mike replied.

"What's the point now? Nature has gone against us. And now I'm not sure we'll be able to come back from it."

"It just needs a few more tweaks. We are literally a few steps away from millions of dollars, Cal."

The man's eyes widened. "Now he knows my name! Gah!"

Ryan watched on, noticing the tension between Mike and Cal. If he could tough it out and be patient, it was likely that the two men would just end up killing each other and that would solve the issue. At that moment, the attention was off him, but as soon as he moved an inch, the focus would be right back on him. He now knew too much and the only way to get out of here safely was to sneak away. Other than that, he was a dead man.

"Can't you just turn the system off?" Ryan asked, unable to keep silent for too long. "Wouldn't that stop the antennas from sending atoms and electricity up into the atmosphere?"

Cal turned on his heel, facing Ryan, his grin turning into a loud laugh, much like an evil scientist. The man wasn't amused in the least bit – he was annoyed, and apparently, Ryan's suggestion was too simple of a fix that wasn't going to work.

"We can't just turn it off! Don't you get it? If we completely stop sending the electrodes up, the atmosphere will backfire. Just think of it in terms of medicine. You take a daily pill every day for months... hell, even years. The doctor doesn't take you off it cold turkey or your body will spaz. It's the same with the atmosphere."

Ryan scoffed and shifted his weight. "I don't see how this could get any worse than it already is."

"I wouldn't say that. You've only seen a very minute section of what the weather has been doing in your little nook in Texas. You haven't even begun to scratch the surface of what our little project has done to the rest of the country and probably the rest of the world. And besides, we are under contract. We have to keep these machines running for as long as we signed on or we don't get paid."

"Or you don't get paid?" Ryan repeated, disbelief obvious in his tone of voice. "You're worried about a damn paycheck after everything that has happened? You're responsible for the deaths of millions and billions of people! You're responsible for almost killing off all of mankind. And you're standing here, telling me you have to keep these machines on because of a fucking contract?" If anything was going to get him shot, it was his blow-up, but he didn't care. He couldn't believe what he was witnessing.

"We are close to getting this right where we need it. Then it's complete security for the United States." Mike finally spoke up again. "I wish you could understand it, Ryan. The power of knowing you can spawn off tornadoes during a super-cell thunderstorm. Or you can completely shut rain off for months on end. And let's not forget tsunamis. It's population control."

"You call killing off almost 95 percent of mankind population control? You have completely lost your mind!"

"We didn't mean for that to happen. But once we get it right where we need it, that will be how it is. We can get the population back up. It's just trial and error."

"Something tells me you can shut these antennas off any time you want. None of this 'weaning the atmosphere' bullshit you just fed me. Where's the power switch, huh? How do you get these things to completely shut down?" Ryan took a step forward and both men lifted their guns, aimed right at Ryan's head.

"Don't take another step," Cal yelled, his index finger resting on the trigger of his revolver. "You touch any of these machines and I make sure you die a slow and painful death, do you understand me?"

Ryan held his hands up, stopping in mid-step. "You two have got to realize the damage you've caused. Is it really worth the money? Mike, you lost your wife. You lost your family. For a paycheck?"

Mike shook his head, his smile wide. "No, Ryan, that's where you're wrong. It's not for the money. It's not for the paycheck. It's for the power! It's for the thrill of being able to play God. And that's exactly what we're doing. Just think of it as thinning out the herd. Those who couldn't make it are gone. Those who have are the strong ones. We'll come back better than ever – a superior human race that can make it through anything."

Ryan took a deep breath. There was still so much to ask, so much to figure out, but he wasn't in a spot to ask many more questions. Both men in front of him were completely insane. The only way he stood a remote chance of making it out of this was to play it cool, do what they said, and eventually catch them off guard. If he continued to press them, it was like pouring salt in an open wound, and eventually one of them would get tired of dealing with him.

"So, what's next?" Ryan asked.

"Take him back to the cabin. Tie him up in the basement. I've got work to get done and I'm not sure what I want to do with him yet." Cal squinted his eyes, still unwilling to lower his gun. "This isn't over, Ryan Gibson. We're not letting you loose. I just feel like you might be valuable to us in some way."

Ryan didn't say a word as Mike handcuffed his hands behind his back, shoving him forward. Losing his balance, he fell to the ground, his body fighting the attempt he made to get back to a standing position.

"Get your ass up, Ryan!" Mike pulled on the cuffs, the hard metal digging into the fresh wounds from where the ropes had burned him. "I hate how it is ending between us."

"You did this, Mike. I don't feel a bit of sympathy for you.

You did all of this. All the people who are dead are on your head. Every single one of them."

Mike didn't respond as he unlocked the cabin and opened the door that exposed a steep set of steps that went down into the dark basement. Ryan had a feeling he'd never see the light of day again. This was likely where he'd die. He thought about Cecilia and Ryan. He wondered what Steve and his father were up to. Eventually, they'd all be dead too. There just weren't enough resources to keep them alive for much longer, despite their attempts at getting Harper Springs back to some type of normalcy.

"Don't worry about Cecilia. She'll make me a good wife." Mike grinned again, not even looking like the same man Ryan had known before.

"Fuck you, Mike. Fuck! You!" Ryan yelled, his anger reaching the highest level he had ever felt. If he wasn't cuffed and restrained, he would've been capable of killing Mike.

"I don't think you're in a place to be talking to me that way."

Mike shoved him down the stairs and Ryan toppled over several, his body collapsing onto the hard floor with a loud thud. Pain shot through his entire body and the metallic flavor was heavy on his tongue again. The last thing he thought about was Cecilia and then everything went completely black around him.

CHAPTER TWENTY-THREE

Steve had to remind himself to keep the pace slow. His instincts were screaming at him, telling him they were close. During all this survival, he had learned to try to listen to what his gut was telling him better than he had when they had technology to rely on. It helped that Darryl had spotted the R and G carved into the tree – if it wasn't for that, he'd still be extremely apprehensive about the direction they were headed.

Going down the snow-covered incline was challenging – the horses continued to fight against them, their hooves unable to gain traction on the slick slope. As smooth as the snow appeared with no tracks to be seen, Ryan had probably been caught in an avalanche. Steve was from Oklahoma where it was mostly flat – he didn't have experience with skiing or any type of mountainous conditions in the wintertime. But then again, neither had Ryan – this area of Texas rarely saw enough snow to even allow skiing, much fewer walls of it rushing down the sides of mountains.

Darryl's horse was matching his step for step, and though every fiber in his being was telling him to hurry, they couldn't push it or they'd both tumble downward, and it was still high enough that they probably wouldn't survive it. Keeping the horses safe was important too – Steve wasn't sure what they'd stumble across when they got down to flat land again.

Ryan could be injured. If he truly was involved in an avalanche, they would have to hurry and get him back to Harper Springs for medical attention. They still couldn't travel fast with the horses, but it'd at least be quicker than hauling him on foot. With the random blizzards and ice storms, none of them would ever make it back alive, all three of them freezing to death.

And Mike Rayburn was also something to consider. What if he was completely hostile and came after them? Steve liked his chances of survival much better if he could run a horse away from the situation.

"It looks like we're almost to the bottom," Darryl said, pointing downward. "The snow is getting a little rougher, meaning it all piled up where the avalanche hit."

Steve couldn't keep himself from going faster, quickening the pace of the horse. When they got off the incline, he circled where Darryl was talking about. More tracks appeared, signaling that whoever was involved in the collapse of snow had probably survived. He surveyed the footprints, confirming that they were two different sets of boots, and they matched the ones that had stopped at the top of the hill.

"Would you look at that!" Darryl gasped and when Steve finally saw what he was looking at, he had the same reaction.

"Are we seriously seeing this? A valley with absolutely no snow?" Steve had to blink to make sure he wasn't dreaming or hallucinating. "What in the hell is going on?"

"I thought with all of this I have seen it all, but this is something else. It's like a secret land that only certain people know about. Is this where we need to rebuild? Was that what Mike was trying to show Ryan?"

"I don't know but this is too strange. How in the hell can that be possible?" Steve rode the horse closer, seeing the valley dipped below them. "I wish I had some binoculars. It looks like there is something fenced in with razor wire."

Darryl put his hand on Steve's shoulder right as he went to move closer. "Whoa. Do you see razor wire? You can't tell what is inside the fence?"

"No, I need to get closer."

"Something tells me we should probably be careful. Why would they have something in razor wire? This all seems strange. And how can this one valley have dodged the weather? There's a cabin on the other side – not one single structure survived the tornadoes."

"Could they have rebuilt one?" Steve asked. "They've had months to do it."

"They could have but it looks like it is in pristine condition. Where in the hell did they get the material to build something like that when everyone's supplies got wiped off the face of the earth?" Darryl clicked his tongue and stared down at the mystery before them. "I don't know about this... And I'm still not sure how Mike and Ryan would tie into it. We need to find out what is inside that fence. That'll probably answer some of our questions."

"We just can't be spotted. We'll probably have to wait until tonight to try and get closer. With their rebuilding capabilities, whoever is doing this is keeping a good watch on everything. If we get caught, we're all as good as dead."

Backtracking toward the hill again, they found a crevice where they could rest and be somewhat hidden. Due to their lack of knowledge of what was happening, they couldn't be too careful when it came to technology and what was readily available. It would've been very easy to step right into a trap and then they'd never be able to save Ryan and figure out what was going on.

Due to it being wintertime, the days were shorter so they wouldn't have to wait too long. During their time waiting, Steve tried to watch if anyone was coming or going, or if any activity was happening in general. He was completely confused about how they could be untouched and how everything around them was covered in snow, appearing like the ice age.

There was a truck that weaved in and out of rows that spread out for acres. Since they were so far away, Steve couldn't tell what the area was made up of, except that it looked like small towers. If they could get closer, he might be able to get a better look, but it still didn't explain all the other questions.

"Look at that!" Darryl pointed up to the sky. The sun was going down in the west but there was still enough light to notice the clouds right above the clear area.

Streaks of white cascaded across the blue, and the setting sun lent an orange hue, making it look like a painting. For a second, Steve forgot where they were and what was going on around them. He took a second to admire the view, his mouth dropping open at the sight. They were cirrus clouds, blanketing just right above the small, clear area.

After a few minutes, the streaks swirled together, blending into large, gray clouds. The wind picked up and the temperature began to dip. As it progressed into a winter storm, it pushed off to the east, away from the antennas, toward where he and Darryl were. Within seconds the sun was covered, and it got as dark as night, aside from the light beaming up from the cabin and mystery farm where they suspected Ryan was.

"Move west, Darryl! It'll get us out from under this system!"

Steve got on his horse, and it neighed and bucked, sending him back against the hard snow. Unwilling to let that slow him down, he hopped back up, grabbing the horse's reins before the animal could escape. Hopping back on, he gained control, both men riding down the hill again, being spotted neither of their concerns right now.

Just a few short yards and they'd be out from under the weather. Lightning flashed between the clouds and a loud clap of thunder echoed and shook the ground. And to Steve's surprise, the antenna farm was unscathed, like it was the most perfect place on the planet to be. And how were there lights on in the cabin? Were the antennas, or whatever the hell they were, being used for electricity? Was this where they needed to relocate to survive?

They got as close as they could to the fence lined with razor wire, getting their first up-close view of the antennas. Steve had no idea what they were looking at – what was this, a movie?"

"They look like poles with helicopter blades on top," Darryl observed. "And it's secure. No one would be able to get through this razor wire."

Steve was afraid to even touch the chain link fence. What if it was electrified and zapped him? Keeping a few feet away, he heard the hum from the antennas and looked up, the sky completely clear, the blue replaced by a blanket of stars. Nightfall was on them but whoever was staying in the cabin hadn't gone to bed yet – every light seemed to be on and if they wanted to find Ryan, they'd eventually have to run across someone who could give them some information.

"How could this..." Steve trailed off, continuing to study the antennas. "Darryl, I think someone is controlling the weather." It sounded insane once he said it out loud, but it was the only conclusion he could come up with.

"What makes you think that?" the older man asked, getting closer to the fence than Steve was comfortable with.

"Did you see what happened? A perfect blue sky transitioned from beautiful cirrus clouds to a massive wall of winter weather that quickly shifted east, away from right here. And look at this place – there's no chance in hell they were hit by any of the tornadoes. There's no way they could've rebuilt all of this with the limited supply and lack of time. Not with the way the weather has been hindering everything we've tried to do."

"How is that even possible?"

"I don't know, but I think these weird-looking metal poles with helicopter blades might have a little to do with it."

Darryl cocked his head to the side as he looked at the machinery that Steve was referring to. "But, why? Why would anyone want to cause the damage and death that this is if your assumption is correct about what is happening?"

"I don't know, Darryl. I'm hoping we'll find out shortly." Steve patted the mane on his horse and took a deep breath. This was going to take courage, but he had to do it for Ryan. And something deep inside told him this went a lot deeper than saving their friend and son. This was to save all of what was left of mankind. "Darryl, how much ammunition do you have on you at this moment? We're going to need every bit of what you have."

❄

RYAN WOKE UP TO DARKNESS. Any time he moved, his head pounded to the rhythm of his pulse, and when he realized he was alone in an unknown place, his heart raced, accentuating the horrible pain that shot down his neck and into his spine. Licking his lips, they felt cracked, and very little moisture was on his tongue. There was a stale taste in his mouth and his body instantly craved water.

Due to the dark, he was disoriented. Where was he and how long had he been there? Crawling on the floor, he attempted to get into a sitting position, which made his head hurt even worse, making him dizzy. He fought vertigo, closing his eyes to get the world to stop spinning. He had to get a handle on things – he needed his memory to come back so he could figure out exactly what was going on with him.

His arms were handcuffed behind his back, the metal digging into his wrists. His shoulders ached from the awkward position he had been laying in, and as he sat up, the strain on his muscles made it almost impossible to do anything other than stay lying on the dirty floor beneath him. Finally maneuvering into a somewhat comfortable position, Ryan leaned his head back against the wall, thankful he was able to find a spot up next to one.

Trying to rehash the last few hours, Ryan's memory finally

came back, hitting him blindside. He was stuck in the badlands of New Mexico at an apparent weather manipulation farm that Mike had been a part of. The helicopter-like antennas, the perfect weather, and the acres of metal poles where the controlling of the atmosphere took place. And Mike's harsh words about Cecilia – right before Ryan was shoved down the steps into the cave of darkness.

The thought of what was transpiring right above him made his anger flare. All for money. All for power. And for them to work with another country made it even worse – Mike was a traitor, plain and simple. And Ryan thought he knew the man. How could he be capable of such evil? Ryan wondered how the man was able to sleep at night, knowing that millions of people had died by his hand. If they wiped out the entire population, where would they even be able to spend the money?

He had to try and find a way out. There was no telling how long he had been locked up and what he and the other man had been up to. His name escaped Ryan – Calvin? It started with a C, but his name was the least of Ryan's worries.

Kicking his legs out in front of him, he forced himself to a standing position, ignoring every one of his body's warnings to sit still. Standing made the other injuries obvious – his back ached, his legs felt like noodles, and of course, the pounding headache that wouldn't go away. He feared a concussion but just like the other man's name, that wasn't his worry. His worry was getting out of the dark room and stopping Mike and the other guy from doing even more damage.

He had no gun or any type of weapon – Mike had been diligent about taking all of that away from him. The only thing he might be able to get away with was escaping and trying to get back to Harper Springs to bring back more manpower, but the idea of trekking back through the snow and ice was daunting. He didn't have a horse anymore so it would all have to be accomplished on foot, and with his current health conditions, he probably wouldn't make it back alive.

There wasn't another option. No matter what he decided to do, he'd be a dead man. If he stayed there, he would have to take on Mike and his friend with his bare hands, likely losing that battle. And if he went back to Harper Springs, he'd die when the next cold front blew in.

Ryan tried hard not to panic. He began to pace, his hands still bound by the metal cuffs. With each second that passed, his heart raced, his head pounded, and he contemplated his very few options. This wasn't going to work. He wasn't going to get out in time to save the people who were lucky enough to still be alive. Or maybe they weren't lucky – maybe they were all better off succumbing to the deteriorating conditions around them. They had all suffered enough.

Leaning against the wall again, his back slid down it until he was in a sitting position again. Ducking his head, he closed his eyes. Both Cecilia's and Ty's faces flashed before him. He couldn't give up. He couldn't let it end like this.

The door at the top of the steps squeaked open and a bright light seeped in, hindering Ryan from being able to see who was standing at the top. Their silhouette looked a lot like Mike's but until the man spoke, he would have to assume that was who it was.

"Get your ass up, Ryan. I've got a few things to show you before I kill you."

CHAPTER TWENTY-FOUR

Steve and Darryl edged closer to the cabin. It wasn't inside of the fence where the mysterious antennas were kept but with the lights on, they were able to see right inside. There were two men in the living room, but they weren't close enough to be able to tell who they were.

Steve slid off his horse and tied it to a tree. Though it wasn't comforting to think about leaving his means of transportation behind, they'd be able to hide a lot easier if they weren't high up on one. Darryl followed suit, both men slouching low as they stepped even closer to the cabin. Sweat dripped down into Steve's eyes, burning them, which was odd considering the winter wasteland that surrounded them in all directions.

They had no real plan for what they were going to do. They weren't even sure if Ryan was in the house. They could at least corner whoever was in the living room and try to get answers out of them. The world they lived in now meant every man for themselves – there were no laws, no cops, and if they wanted to hold someone at gunpoint they could. There would be no aggravated assault charges, no hearings, and most of all, no prison time. It was good to know that, but it was also scary to know that. Anarchy was exploding everywhere, and the good, honest people were stuck right in the middle of it.

There was talking going on, but it was a murmur, muffled by the walls that separated them from inside. They were close enough now to the cabin to touch it, and Steve took a deep breath, glancing over at Darryl who looked calm. How could he be? This was an intense situation and neither of them knew how it would play out.

Clenching his fists, Steve felt the heavy weight of the gun in his pocket. Should he go ahead and draw it now to have it ready? That could be a huge mistake. What if he got trigger-happy and shot at the first sign of danger, accidentally hitting Ryan? He couldn't allow himself to make such a futile mistake.

"When do you want to make a move?" Darryl asked, his voice low that Steve almost didn't hear him.

"I guess there's not a perfect time to go in there."

"I think I heard Ryan's voice."

"Which means we have to be careful. They could go crazy and just start shooting. Or he could be hit by friendly fire."

Darryl nodded, clenching his jaw as he peered through the window. "He's in there. So is Mike."

"Do they look like they are arguing?" Steve asked, trying to get a better idea of the scene playing out in front of them.

"No, but Ryan's hands are cuffed behind his back."

"Shit..." Steve muttered. "We better move before they take him somewhere. What about guns or weapons?"

"I can't tell. Mike's back is to me." Darryl ducked quickly, making Steve follow. He didn't say anything, but his eyes moved up toward the window, letting Steve know that they needed to be completely quiet and still. Steve tried to steady his breathing – they couldn't allow a stupid mistake to ruin the progress they had made in locating Ryan.

"I'm ready to make a move when you are, Darryl," Steve whispered. "No more playing around. Let's do this."

❄

RYAN STOOD in the living room, his eyes staying on the two guns pointing at him. Cal and Mike both had one on them and at any second, Ryan predicted one would lose his cool or nerve and pull the trigger, seriously hurting Ryan or mortally wounding him. He felt his heartbeat in his chest, so hard that he feared he would eventually have a heart attack from the strain on the organ.

"Why is it so important to you to show him how this works?" Cal asked Mike, looking from him back to Ryan.

"Just thought it'd be interesting. Besides, he won't be able to use it, anyway. He's a dead man walking. Just thought he might enjoy the last thirty or so minutes of his life learning about something he'll never be able to fix. And so he'll know what his precious family will be dealing with for the rest of their lives."

The mention of Cecilia and Ty made Ryan want to attack them, but the odds were against him. Two guns against him were unarmed and he was also handcuffed behind his back. He didn't stand a chance of even hurting one of them before they would be able to get a shot off on him.

"Look at him, not even saying anything. This is the quietest I've ever seen you, Ryan." Mike mocked him, patting him on the cheek. "Like I said earlier, I'll take real good care of Cecilia for you."

Ryan clenched his jaw. There was no need to stoop to Mike's level. He needed to figure out a way to get out of this, but nothing was coming to mind. If he ran, he wouldn't get far on foot, especially without the use of his arms and hands.

"Shut up, Mike! Let's get him out there and get this over with. I've got to try and call back in – no one is answering their phone anymore and I'm wondering if one of these last systems we brewed up killed off our allies." Cal paced, raking his hand through his hair, his brow tense. "If that's the case, there goes our paycheck. There goes our main source of income."

"Then stop while you're ahead," Ryan replied.

Cal looked him in the eye, a smirk forming on his lips. "You gotta be kidding me. It's not just the money I'm liking. It's the power. And I'm not going to stop. We are safe here. As you can see, a piece of land untouched, free for us to do what we need."

"And what good is it if you have wiped out the entire population on Earth?"

"That's where Cecilia comes in," Mike laughed, shoving Ryan backward against the door. "Now get your ass moving. We need to get this over with. You're nothing but a hiccup in our master plan."

Ryan walked backward until Mike turned him around, both men directly behind him as they walked toward the pasture where the weather control antennas were. The hum got louder as they approached, and Ryan felt the bile rise in the back of his throat. His hands felt sweaty, and he balled up his fists, feeling the cold metal dig into his already damaged skin. This couldn't be happening. After everything they had gone through, all the rebuilding and planning, only for him to finally get a glimpse of what was going on, an answer for everything he had questioned, to be killed, leaving Cecilia and Ty left behind to suffer.

They walked past several antennas until Mike grabbed Ryan's arm, stopping him in mid-step. He patted the metal pole, the hum even louder now that they were standing right under one. It appeared bigger than when Ryan initially saw them and from all the wiring and construction, it had to have taken a genius to figure out how to get such a thing built and working correctly.

Cal circled it, looking up at the blades in admiration, his smile wide. "The ions build up inside here." He pointed to the larger part of the cylinder. "They build up and shoot the electricity up into the atmosphere. It responds with the ionosphere, developing massive supercell thunderstorms and winter weather events. It also has the power to completely clean out the air, which in turn caused the drought and high temperatures that came right before winter. It caused a high-pressure system, which hindered any type of rain or system to even form."

"Do you decide what type of weather it does?" Ryan asked, though he didn't want to know. What good would this information do him now?

"We're working on that but haven't got it fine-tuned just yet."

"By the way this got out of hand, it doesn't look like you've gotten any of it fine-tuned," Ryan said, not even feeling the need to hold back anymore. As Mike had said, he was a dead man walking.

Mike backhanded him across the face, jolting any previous injuries, the pain searing through Ryan. He felt warmth trickle on his lip, reopening the gash on it.

Cal smiled again, though it wasn't from amusement. It had evil written all over it – he had no regard for other human life. The money and power had blinded him.

"The ionosphere responds to the electricity depending on what season we're in. Springtime led to tornadoes, summer was bad temperatures and no rain, and now here we are in winter. It did make winter come earlier than usual due to the overload of additions in the atmosphere."

Ryan took a deep breath and licked his lip, tasting the blood again. "Who taught you all of this? How did you know how to do it?"

Cal shrugged and looked toward Mike. "I'm ex-military. We talked about weather control all the time. Meteorological warfare was a big topic, we just never actually did it. When I got out, I ran with the idea. Other countries were for it. I finally got enough funding from interested parties and the rest is history."

"And you planned to completely kill everyone? I bet those interested parties are dead along with everyone else. How's that for a good plan?" Ryan cringed, expecting another slap from Mike but it didn't come.

"Like I said, we are working on it. But with those interested parties out of the way, we are on top. Nothing can touch us now."

Ryan went to ask another question, but Mike cut him off.

"Okay, enough talking. The sooner we get you taken care of, the sooner I can get Cecilia back here and start repopulating the planet." He shoved Ryan and it took everything he had to keep his balance. Vertigo hit him and he was able to stay standing, knowing that wouldn't last long.

"Get on your knees!" Cal yelled, the echo of his voice sounding like it carried for miles.

Ryan hesitated but did as he was told, kneeling on the hard ground in front of both men. He looked up at Mike, right in the eyes. "You used to be a respectable man, Mike. A good chief that I loved working under."

"Shut the hell up! Your guilt trip isn't going to talk me out of this!" Mike held the gun up, the barrel point blank against the top of Ryan's head. "Any last words before I off you? Anything you want to tell your wife?"

The metal barrel was pushing into Ryan's scalp and he could think of a million things he wanted to say, none that were Mike or Cal's business. Hopefully, she knew what was heavy on his heart.

"Tell her I love her."

With that last statement, Ryan squinted his eyes closed as two gunshots rang out. He didn't feel any pain. When he opened his eyes, he was right where he had knelt just minutes before. Mike was sprawled out in front of him, his eyes wide open, staring up at the sky. Cal was in almost the same position, both men shot in the head, their glossy expressions confirming that they were dead.

He tried to get up off his knees and figure out exactly what had happened. He felt someone's hand help him to a standing position and his heart skipped a beat when he saw both his father and Steve by his side.

"I've never been happier to see you two than I am right now," Ryan said, feeling a natural grin on his lips. "What brings you by?"

Steve kicked the guns away from both men even though it

was pretty apparent that they wouldn't be able to use them ever again. "Decided to show up just in time. So, what did you learn about these things?" Steve patted the pole that Cal had just been pacing around, informing Ryan of their capabilities.

"That they need to be turned off and demolished," Ryan replied as Darryl dug for the handcuff key, finding it in the jacket pocket that Mike was wearing. Freeing him from the restraints felt amazing and he rubbed each wrist, the soreness a dull ache compared to his pounding head.

"And how do we go about doing that?" Steve asked, looking over the gauges and switches.

"He didn't get that far in teaching me but I'm sure between the three of us, we can figure it out." Ryan patted his jeans, remembering they had taken all his belongings, including his pocketknife. "Either of you have a knife on you? I bet we can start by cutting the wires." Their theory was working – with each wire cut the low hum stopped and that was enough evidence to know that the weather control machines would not be sending any more electricity up into the ionosphere.

Steve went to work, disabling each antenna across the pasture. Darryl patted Ryan on the shoulder and looked down at the ground. "I didn't think I'd ever see you again." His voice cracked and he quickly wiped something from his face.

"Me either, Dad. I was for sure I was a goner and the rest of y'all would be left behind to deal with this."

"You think there's anyone else involved?"

Ryan nodded and watched Steve – the man was enjoying his task of disabling all the antennas, a bounce in his step as he went from tower to tower, shutting them down. "Probably. But we'll be ready for them if they come around."

"You're sure about that?" Darryl asked, his smile accompanied by a laugh.

"You're damn right I am. After everything we've all been through, I don't think anything is going to stop us from building a decent future for those of us who remain. We just have to keep an eye on the looters and make sure we're protected from a possible attack. That threat still exists."

"So, they were controlling the weather, huh?" Darryl's father clicked his tongue and shook his head. "And Mike Rayburn was directly involved. You think you know a person." He paused, taking a swig from his canteen before offering it to Ryan, who took it and drank most of its contents. "You're going to have to fill me in on everything they told you," Darryl said, his eyes remaining downcast.

"Looks like the weather around us is already improving. The wind has stopped blowing and the sun is coming up." Ryan handed his father the canteen. "We've got a long hike back to Harper Springs. I'll tell y'all all about it on the way home."

WANT MORE DISASTER SURVIVAL THRILLERS?

Check out the Respect the Wind Series!

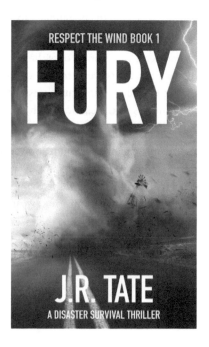

In this war waged on a grand scale, families are torn apart, communities shattered, and the very fabric of civilization unravels. With dwindling resources and desperate stakes, Gavin and Avery must delve into the depths of scientific knowledge to comprehend the origins of these apocalyptic weather patterns. Yet, as they uncover shocking truths, they face a haunting realization—nature is gearing up for its ultimate revenge, poised to reclaim what was once taken for granted and usher in the extinction of the human race.

Amid the chaos, Gavin and Avery must summon their expertise, courage, and unyielding determination to defy the unfathomable forces of nature. Can they unlock the secrets that lie within the tempests' heart and find a way to preserve humanity's existence? Or will they become mere witnesses to the earth's wrathful retribution?

In this gripping tale of suspense and survival, the boundaries of human ingenuity are tested against the overwhelming power of nature. Brace yourself for an electrifying journey as Gavin and Avery navigate a world teetering on the edge of annihilation, where the ultimate question looms: Can humanity outwit its own demise and weather the storm of a lifetime?

ACKNOWLEDGMENTS

I have to begin by thanking all of the readers out there! Without you, this would be like I was talking to myself. I hope you enjoyed The Damaged Climate Series as much as I enjoyed writing it. There is always a possibility of a book four in the series but I also ended it where it wasn't a massive cliffhanger. Secondly, I have to thank my mother, Patti, who has been so supportive of my writing endeavors. She listens to my griping, my ideas, and everything in between. Without her, I don't think I could ever finish a book! Thanks again to all of you who have taken the time to read my work and give me feedback, whether it is through emails, social media, or by reviews on the product page. It's always rewarding to hear what people think of my work. And last but not least, I have to send a huge shout out to Leslie Goodfellow, the kind lady who took the time to help with edits! Her suggestions and watchful eye helped improve the quality of the manuscript. You are the best!

ABOUT THE AUTHOR

J.R. Tate is an accomplished author based in Texas, where she draws inspiration from the breathtaking landscapes and the spirit of resilience that permeates the region. With a passion for nature and adventure, she often explores the great outdoors, hiking through scenic trails and finding solace in the mountains. These experiences lend an authentic touch to her writing, bringing the settings and landscapes to life with vivid detail.

Beyond her literary pursuits, she also works as a social-emotional counselor, dedicated to helping children navigate their emotions and behaviors. Her background in counseling provides her with a deep understanding of the human psyche, which shines through in her compelling character portrayals and exploration of complex emotions.

As an author, J.R. captivates readers with her engaging storytelling and immersive writing style. She seamlessly weaves together elements of suspense, adventure, and human drama, creating narratives that keep readers on the edge of their seats. With each page, she delves into the depths of her characters' hearts, unearthing their fears, hopes, and desires, and inviting readers to embark on emotional journeys alongside them.

Her commitment to crafting compelling stories is matched only by her dedication to authenticity and attention to detail. Her ability to capture the essence of the human experience in the face of adversity resonates deeply with readers, leaving a lasting impact long after they turn the final page.

With her unique blend of adventure, heartfelt emotion, and a keen understanding of the human condition, she is an author to watch. Her stories transport readers to captivating worlds, exploring the triumphs and tribulations of her characters in a way that leaves a lasting impression.

Join my mailing list to get updates on new releases! No spam will be sent!

http://eepurl.com/byKpRb

Email:

JTateAuthor@yahoo.com

Website:

https://jtateauthor.wixsite.com/jrtate

TikTok:

JRTateAuthor

facebook.com/RustyBucketPublishing

twitter.com/JRTateAuthor

instagram.com/j.r.tateauthor

Made in United States
Troutdale, OR
07/12/2023

11151071R00126